Ways to Annoy Joe Malone:

1. Wear that short knit dress to the office—it's just a *bit* too clingy.

2. Read his mail when he's not looking—and deny it when you get caught.

3. Try to figure out if he really *does* have a tattoo...in a personal place.

4. Never, ever let him get the last word—even on those rare occasions when he's right.

5. Under no circumstances admit you've had a thing for him for the past twelve years. A girl's entitled to *some* secrets, after all....

FRIENDS OF
MUNCIE PUBLIC LIBRARY

Dear Reader,

Well, I had to go back—*way* back—to come up with something to talk about this month. All the way back to high school, in fact, when there was this cute substitute teacher. (No, I'm not going to tell you his name—I'm not even sure I still remember it!) I don't think he ever taught my class, but somehow I got to know him. He was only a few years older than mature-senior me, and *cute!* We both wrote poetry, which we let each other read and then discussed. And that was about it. (Except that he did once ask me to make him an artistic sign so he could hitchhike up to Wood's Hole, Massachusetts, to see a friend.) But even though nothing ever happened outside my imagination (I was certain I'd run into him after being away at college, he'd fall madly in love with me and we'd launch ourselves into marriage—yeah, right!), I've never forgotten him. Or, to be honest, his name—I'm just not telling.

And the book that brought back this spate of memories? *The Education of Jake Flynn,* by Leandra Logan. This time she's the teacher and he's the…student. And this time imaginations aren't the only place where things are happening!

Don't miss our second book, either: *Dear Mr. Right,* by Jennifer Drew. Working with Joe Malone—on a dating column, of all things—was not Amy's idea of fun. Or was it? He did have that very personal tattoo.… (Hey, why didn't I think to tell you about mine?)

Until next time—enjoy!

Leslie Wainger

Leslie Wainger
Senior Editor and Editorial Coordinator

Please address questions and book requests to:
Silhouette Reader Service
U.S.: 3010 Walden Ave., P.O. Box 1325, Buffalo, NY 14269
Canadian: P.O. Box 609, Fort Erie, Ont. L2A 5X3

JENNIFER DREW

Dear Mr. Right

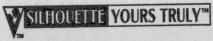

Published by Silhouette Books
America's Publisher of Contemporary Romance

If you purchased this book without a cover you should be aware that this book is stolen property. It was reported as "unsold and destroyed" to the publisher, and neither the author nor the publisher has received any payment for this "stripped book."

To the next generation of Mr. Rights:
Andrew and Tyler

 SILHOUETTE BOOKS

ISBN 0-373-52028-X

DEAR MR. RIGHT

Copyright © 1996 by Pamela Hanson and Barbara Andrews

All rights reserved. Except for use in any review, the reproduction or utilization of this work in whole or in part in any form by any electronic, mechanical or other means, now known or hereafter invented, including xerography, photocopying and recording, or in any information storage or retrieval system, is forbidden without the written permission of the editorial office, Silhouette Books, 300 East 42nd Street, New York, NY 10017 U.S.A.

All characters in this book have no existence outside the imagination of the author and have no relation whatsoever to anyone bearing the same name or names. They are not even distantly inspired by any individual known or unknown to the author, and all incidents are pure invention.

This edition published by arrangement with Harlequin Books S.A.

® and TM are trademarks of Harlequin Books S.A., used under license. Trademarks indicated with ® are registered in the United States Patent and Trademark Office, the Canadian Trade Marks Office and in other countries.

Printed in U.S.A.

About the author

JENNIFER DREW IS:

A. Girl detective Nancy Drew's evil twin

B. Joe Malone's ex-girlfriend

C. Silhouette's mother-daughter writing team of Barbara Andrews and Pam Hanson

If you answered C., congratulations!

Barbara is the bestselling author of twenty-one romances under her own name. Pam is a former journalist who met her own Mr. Right in the newsroom.

"I love having my daughter as my partner," says Barbara. "Since we teamed up, writing has never been more fun."

Adds Pam, "It's great to give Mom advice for a change! Seriously, people ask how I can work with my mother. It probably helps to live nearly a thousand miles apart, although we often talk on the phone three times a day! Our long-distance bills are terrible, but it's all worth it when readers write to tell us how much they like a book. We'd love to hear what you think of *Dear Mr. Right*. We'd also like to know if you guessed where Joe's tattoo is!"

Please write to:

Jennifer Drew
P.O. Box 4084
Morgantown, WV 26504

Books by Jennifer Drew

Silhouette Yours Truly

Dear Mr. Right

Silhouette Romance

Turn Back the Night #1040

1

Dear Holly Heartfelt,
Six months ago I introduced my best friend to my fiancé. Yesterday she asked me to be a bridesmaid at her wedding—when she marries my ex-fiancé. The dress she wants me to buy costs $500, just the amount I've saved for a vacation at the beach this summer. What should I do?

Torn

Amy Patterson twisted a strand of dark copper hair, forgetting she'd just had it styled in a smooth bob, and stared at the letter on her computer screen.

"You've been burned once—go for the tan this time," she said out loud, testing the tone of the words as a possible response to the question sent to the *Phoenix Monitor*'s advice column.

"Talking to yourself again, Amy?" Melanie Hayes asked, stopping to peer over Amy's shoulder at the reader's question she was working on.

"Didn't anyone teach you it's bad manners to read other people's screens, Melanie?" Amy glared at the willowy blond life-style reporter towering over her like a cross between a high-fashion model and a stork.

"You're certainly touchy. Oh, I remember. You get the word from the powers-that-be today. Will you or won't you be the next Holly Heartfelt? What an outdated name. Really, Amy, why do you want the job?''

''It pays the rent,'' Amy mumbled, unwilling to bare her soul to a reporter who thought in-depth coverage meant the person being interviewed had a swimming pool.

She pretended to reread the letter on her screen until Melanie wandered off to annoy someone else.

''Dear Torn,'' Amy wrote, imagining the nervy bride-to-be was Melanie. ''Here's a multiple-choice question. Pick the answer that best reflects the way you feel:

A. I adore this couple and want them to be my closest friends for life.

B. I resent what they've done to me but want the guests at their wedding to think I'm a good sport.

C. I didn't save for a year so my ex-best friend could heap one more humiliation on me. Look out, beach! Here I come!''

Amy leaned back in her chair and reread what she'd written, feeling a glow of satisfaction. She was right on target on this one. She could smooth it over later—if Bertram Ulysses Garver gave her the job.

Ten minutes later, she was in the managing editor's deserted reception area. Rose, his secretary, spent most of her time at the copy machine down the hall; Garver worked hard to destroy a tree a day by papering the building with memos that were largely ignored.

''You're looking good today.'' Roberta Higuera, a copy editor and Amy's best friend at the paper, poked her head through the open doorway. ''Lunch is my treat—to celebrate your new job.''

''If I get it!'' Amy nervously smoothed the short skirt of her peach linen suit.

''You're a shoo-in after four years as Holly's assistant. Everyone knows you've practically written the whole column for the past year. Oh, Rose told me to tell you to go right in. B.U. is waiting for you." She spoke softly; Garver wouldn't appreciate an employee using his initials. "Good luck!"

Amy checked the wall clock and her watch. Eleven thirty-four. Both were the same, not surprising since every timepiece in the building was synchronized with the replica of Big Ben in the lobby. Since the original London Bridge had been hauled to Arizona from England years before, some interior decorators had come up with weird ideas. She hurried to the door of the only office in the building not walled with glass.

"You're four minutes late, Patterson," Bertram Garver said when she hesitantly pushed open the heavy oak door.

The managing editor dressed to intimidate. Although he'd lived in Phoenix for nearly twenty years, he tried to look like an Eastern bank president: charcoal pin-striped suit, starched white shirt, silver-and-onyx cuff links and a good-old-boy school tie in somber shades of burgundy and gray. Even his balding pate suggested spit and polish. He made Amy feel wrinkled and untucked. She had to fight a tendency to keep her eyes focused on the floor whenever she talked to him, which fortunately wasn't often.

"Sorry, Mr. Garver. I was working on the column, and time slipped..." She let the end of her sentence trail off when she noticed a pair of well-oiled brown boots attached to long chino-clad legs.

"Amy, I'd like you to meet someone."

Garver using her first name was a sure sign of disaster: a pat on the back from a hangman.

"This is—"

"Joe Malone!" She unintentionally interrupted her boss, blurting out the name of the man who turned around when introduced.

"Amy—Amy Patterson?" A tall, lean, dark-haired man studied her with azure blue eyes, a leisurely stare that took in everything from the top of her head to her toes.

This was one man she would recognize when he was ninety. His deep, mellow voice had been distinctive even when he was a teenager, and the fine sun-wrinkles at the corners of his eyes only made him more handsome in a mature, heart-stopping way. She was looking forward with trepidation to turning thirty in two years, but he made the big 3-0 look positively appealing.

"You two already know each other?" Garver asked, sounding mildly irritated, as though they'd robbed him of delivering a carefully prepared introduction.

"I went to high school with an Amy Patterson," Joe said with a teasing grin, "and I'm pretty sure I recognize that hair color."

She'd worked for years to leave the high school Amy behind her—a short, chunky girl with braces on her teeth and wild, frizzy red hair. Under his all-knowing scrutiny, she felt her body bloating, her teeth unstraightening and her expensive bob kinking up.

"Actually, Mr. Garver, Joe and my brother went to school together. I was two grades behind."

Explaining made her feel even more awkward, and it was all Joe's fault for being such a hunk—then and now. She hadn't been in his league when it came to the dating game, and here he was, a dozen years later, still making her feel like queen of the nerds. She gave herself a mental kick in the behind and tilted her chin at a haughty angle, hoping her momentary lapse of confidence was only nervousness about her job future.

"I'm pleased you two know each other," Garver said in his take-charge voice, "since you'll be working together."

"Not again!" Amy exclaimed.

"What do you mean?" Garver asked, obviously losing patience because the meeting wasn't following his script.

"Bert, we worked on our high school newspaper together," Joe announced before she could explain.

He called Bertram Ulysses Garver by a nickname! Just what the newsroom needed, a new writer who was pals with the boss!

"I was the editor," Joe went on, not noticing her chagrin. "Amy was one of my little reporters."

He draped his arm casually around her shoulders and hugged her close. She wanted to sock him!

"I don't understand, Mr. Garver." She pulled free of Joe's heavy arm. "I've done most of the work on the column since Holly's health problems began. Are you unhappy with my work?"

"Not at all, or you wouldn't be in the picture, Amy. You've been doing a very competent job, but we're redesigning the format of the advice column, giving it 'his' and 'her' viewpoints. We want to target younger readers—the ones our advertisers are courting—without losing the hardcore older readers, of course."

Amy shook her head, still too much in shock to rally any arguments against the idea. She'd been Holly Gordon's assistant for four long years, starting as a letter sorter, progressing from opening envelopes and doing research to writing most of the column herself. She didn't deserve to have it snatched away from her!

"We hope to distribute the revamped column through our own syndicate—assuming, of course, that the new format is successful," Garver explained. "We hired Joe to give us an extra edge on the competition."

Amy controlled her urge to scream and tried to rearrange the features on her face into something resembling intelligent thoughtfulness.

"I'm still a little confused, Mr. Garver," she said. "Advice is a specialty. It's not like hard news where you just report what's happening. It takes experience, sensitivity—"

"I was working part-time on an advice column in Minneapolis, along with covering the police beat," Joe interrupted. "Both involved a lot of dysfunctional relationships, so they aren't as far apart as you might think," he said, reaching over to flick aside a strand of hair that had fallen over her eye.

She wanted to slap his hand; she wanted to throttle Bertie "Bug" Garver. All kinds of primitive urges were bubbling up, and she imagined herself doing something evil, like messing up the precise pile of papers on the gleaming glass top of the managing editor's ultraneat desk.

Worse, she could feel heat in her cheeks. Her face was probably the awful strawberry pink shade that had gotten her so much teasing in her school days.

"This is a new concept, and Joe's experience will go a long way in developing it," Garver said, standing to indicate he was too busy to listen to objections. "I think you'll be happy with your new contract, Amy. We'll go over the terms after you've had a chance to look at it. Legal will get it to you soon. In the meantime, Joe can brief you on all the details we've discussed."

"He's in charge of the column?" She didn't recognize her voice; it sounded squeaky.

"No, it's a fifty-fifty arrangement for now. If it goes well—and I have every confidence in both of you—we'll have you in syndication within a year. It's all spelled out in your contract, Patterson."

Garver fiddled with the small pile of papers on his desk. Amy studied the tips of his black wing tips, distorted by the thick glass top. She imagined she could hear Joe smacking his lips in satisfaction. She glared at him, then quickly averted her eyes.

He was grinning like an inflatable plastic alligator.

"Joe, report to personnel this afternoon. They have some things for you to sign, then they'll give you a tour of the plant. Pleasure having you at the *Monitor*."

"Thank you, Bert. I'm really looking forward to working here."

"Patterson, I have an idea for the column that we'll discuss later. I'm expecting great things from the new format. I trust you'll do your part to ensure that the new format is a success."

"Yes, sir."

She was Patterson again, but the boss called Joe by his first name as if they were old fishing buddies.

"Any other questions?" Garver asked in a tone that dared her to ask one.

"No, sir," she lied, wondering what other bright idea he was going to toss at her when she'd had time to recover from phase one of his disaster plan. What she really needed was advice on dealing with Joe Malone!

Amy felt conspicuous walking through the busy newsroom with Joe. She was determined to hold back what she really wanted to say to him until they didn't have an audience. Several heads turned in their direction, and she could see from the appreciative female glances directed at Joe that he was attracting attention.

"Here's my—our office." She nearly choked on the plural possessive.

"It's intimate." He stepped inside the glass cubicle and made it seem crowded.

"It's small, Joe. In fact, I'm not sure it's big enough for both of us."

"I think it'll be just fine—if you're not territorial."

"Why, sir, are you giving me advice?" she asked in her best imitation of a baby-doll voice.

"Let's cut to the chase—"

"Get down to brass tacks, put our best feet forward, chew the fat—" she offered.

"I'm partial to putting my cards on the table and my boots under the bed, but if you want to draw a chalk line to divide the room—"

"This is my desk," she said, pretending she didn't see his macho smirk. If he thought making a joke out of everything was the way to build a partnership, she knew a comedy club where the audience threw rotten vegetables at bad acts. She pushed aside some clutter and perched on the desk top, crossing one leg over the other.

She had his full attention now. Was that a glint of appreciation as his eyes lingered for several moments on her well-conditioned thighs? She was no femme fatale, but she was prepared to use every weapon in her arsenal to let Joe Malone know she wasn't his little reporter anymore. She wasn't relinquishing control of the column!

"You were never this much of a distraction at good old Horace Mann High."

"That was a long time ago, Joe. I'm not a naive sophomore anymore."

"You were a spunky one. I remember when the school board was planning to remodel the girls' locker room, and you led the fight against it. I wondered at the time why you had a burr under your saddle on that issue."

She was losing control of the conversation! Reminiscing over her ill-fated shower crusade was the last thing she wanted.

"A burr under my saddle? I really would like to read some of the columns you wrote in Minneapolis. Bet the geriatric generation thought you were really hip, cool, the cat's pajamas."

"We're getting off on the wrong . . . I mean, let's make a fresh start here, Amy." He grabbed her hand and gave it a businesslike shake, firm but not bone crushing. "Hello, I'm Joe Malone, your new partner. You haven't asked, but yes, I'm glad to be here in the sunny Southwest again. It gets damn cold in Minnesota."

"Surely you had someone to keep you warm on those frigid Midwestern nights? Oh—none of my business, of course." Her cheeks were feeling hot again, and she remembered Malone, the smart-aleck high school editor, calling her a member of the blush-a-day club.

"Scary as it seems, your future is my future on this paper," he said, no playfulness in his tone now.

Had she hit a nerve, asking if there was someone special in his life?

He leaned toward her, bracing himself by putting one hand on either side of her thighs—which were exposed by the skirt that had ridden up to within inches of her underwear. Sitting on the desk suddenly seemed like a dumb ploy, which made her even madder—at him.

"In order for this column to be a success," he said, "I'm willing to forget the time you changed my byline on an article to Joe Baloney...."

"You never proved it was me! And the column is already a success," she said, trying not to notice the thick, mahogany brown hair curled over the collar of his roughly woven dark olive sports jacket. If he'd ever gotten this close to her in high school, she would have been ecstatic. Now she was just plain agitated. Forget the past, right! Forget he'd played havoc with her adolescent emotions without even noticing she was a girl. Well, she had his full attention now, and she didn't like the reason for it one little bit. "Holly Heartfelt has been one of the top features in the *Phoenix Monitor* for over twenty-two years."

"I know. Holly Gordon did a great job initiating it and writing it all those years, but it's our turn now. So let's make the readers forget it was ever written by a sweet old lady." He made it sound like an order.

"We may be in this together—temporarily—but this time Joe Malone isn't in charge."

"You still don't know how to handle an aggressive male." To Amy's surprise, he laughed and backed away from her. "There's no good reason for your hostility."

"I'm not hostile—just cautious. I know what to expect from you."

"I once had a pet iguana who gave me friendlier welcomes than you have—and all he did was hiss and try to slap me with his tail."

"Keeping exotic animals as pets is a crime against nature," she muttered.

"I think you're still ticked about not being made editor of the high school newspaper when you were a sophomore and I was a senior."

"I'd forgotten all about that."

She could feel her cheeks redden at the memory. She'd nearly convinced the Student Activities Board that she would make a better editor as a sophomore than any senior, especially him. She had been devastated when he got the job, but it had been a long time ago.

"It's only natural you're harboring a residue of resentment toward me now," he said matter-of-factly.

"If this is the kind of psychobabble you pass off as advice, we're doomed."

"If you're not happy sharing the column, you could explore other options."

"I've invested four years in Holly Heartfelt! I'm not walking away from it now."

She was determined not to let him be the winner by default. She hadn't backed down from the fight to edit the school paper, even though it had meant going against the most popular boy in the senior class. She certainly wasn't going to let him deprive her of a job she deserved.

"I've read some of your columns," he said. "They're not bad. You've never read mine, so don't you think your hostility is premature? I might be a great advice giver."

"And you may be an egotistical hack." She was too upset to care what she said. It was her column; she'd never get another opportunity like this again. She wasn't going to relinquish one iota of control to him.

"There's only one way to find out," he challenged her. "Read my work. If you're unhappy working with me after you've read some of my columns, at least your objections will be professional ones.''

"It doesn't have anything to do with whether I want to work with you. I don't think it's a good idea to change a column as popular as Holly Heartfelt's. Since I started doing most of the work, letters have increased nearly twenty percent. Don't think for one minute I'll quit when I have so much effort invested in it.''

"Good. I'd hate to see the new format put on hold while they search for another female writer.''

"I'm meeting a friend for lunch," she said, abruptly ending their discussion and sliding to her feet.

Outside in the newsroom, everyone appeared to be hard at work, eyes riveted to terminals. Even the mail clerk was bent over, elbows propped on a desk, watching a city-beat reporter putting words on a screen. They weren't fooling her! A few seconds earlier, they'd all been practicing their lip-reading skills. Having her own office meant quieter working conditions, but the glass-walled cubicle had the privacy of a fish tank.

Roberta was walking down the long, desk-lined aisle, her shiny patent-leather purse slung over one shoulder. The copy editor's dress was like a Gauguin painting, vivid splashes of color that blended together like jungle blooms. She wore her midnight black hair in bouncy, shoulder-length waves and favored heavy silver jewelry made by Native Americans. Unlike most of the people Amy knew, she was happily married and she and her orthodontist husband had two sons.

Amy walked out to meet her, trying to ignore the soft footfalls that told her Joe was following.

"What's the news?" Roberta asked in a husky whisper.

"I'm still in—sort of. I'll tell you over lunch." All Amy wanted at the moment was to put distance between herself and the *Phoenix Monitor*.

"Honey, I'm sorry. I'll have to give you a rain check. Todd's school called—he's in the nurse's office with a temp of 103. I have to go pick him up, but Melanie is meeting us in the lobby. She asked to come along, and I couldn't think of a reason to say no. Hope you don't mind too much."

Amy groaned inwardly but only nodded at her friend. Of course Melanie wanted to eat with her today—a once-a-year occurrence. She was probably hoping for a chance to gloat because the job had fallen through.

Amy couldn't manage a grin, so she settled for looking inscrutable.

"Hello, I'm Joe Malone." He caught up with Amy and stepped between her and Roberta. "I'll be working on the advice column with Amy."

"Oh." Roberta looked as dumbfounded as Amy had been.

"A new format—his-and-her opinions," Joe went on.

"It's nice to meet you, Mr. Malone. I'm Roberta Higuera, copy editor. Welcome to the *Monitor*."

"Thanks. It's great to be here. Say, can you recommend a good place for lunch—quick service but not fast food?"

He was as subtle as a bulldozer, pretending he didn't know where to find a restaurant in his own hometown.

"I'm standing Amy up, but she's meeting one of the life-style reporters in the lobby," Roberta said, walking into his trap, much to Amy's chagrin. "I'm sure they'd love to have you join them, if you don't mind being outnumbered two to one."

"I like those odds, that is, if you don't mind, Amy."

Melanie picked that moment to appear. "I wondered what was keeping you. I have to beg off lunch. I have to interview some guy who's eighty-something and still hikes the Grand Canyon rim to rim every year. It'll probably take me an hour to find his house in Sun City."

"I hope it's not another cat house," Amy said, taking a cheap shot but not especially proud of it. Melanie was allergic to cats, but a life-style reporter had to go into homes to chase down everyone from mousetrap inventors to carousel-horse collectors. More than once she'd returned to the newsroom with puffy eyes and a red nose, but she claimed to have a phobia about needles and refused to get allergy shots.

"Melanie, this is Joe Malone. He's just starting on the *Monitor*," Roberta said. "Joe, Melanie Hayes. I'll see you all later."

"I'm so pleased to meet you, Joe." Melanie extended both hands, capturing his palm and covering it, letting daggerlike coral nails scrape lightly across his wrist. It was her version of an erotic handshake. The stupid grin on his face wasn't exactly a protest.

The predatory look in her co-worker's eyes gave Amy the creeps, but Joe was old enough to take care of himself. She immediately squelched the little voice in her head that asked, *Jealous, Amy?*

"Well, Amy," Melanie gushed, talking to her but looking at Joe, "what happened in your meeting with Bug?"

"He called me by my first name, waved a contract in my face and—" she smiled maliciously "—gave me Joe."

"Gave you..."

"Joe."

"But..."

"Oh, I know, our office is tiny, but we have two chairs, two screens. What more do partners need?"

"Partners..."

"I'll be giving my usual clear, insightful advice, and Joe will add the male point of view."

"Oh, I get it," Melanie said. "Comic relief from all that heavy moralizing. You're the straight man—"

"And he takes the pratfalls. Isn't that right, Joe?"

He looked ready to throttle her but managed a weak laugh. "I'm available for birthday parties, too."

"Let's get going," Amy said with all the gusto of a drill sergeant.

Joe watched the blonde slink away, then followed Amy down a broad flight of marble stairs to the heavy glass door in the lobby. His welcome had gone from Amy's absolute zero to Melanie's five hundred degrees centigrade, and he already regretted finagling the lunch invitation. His new partner probably needed time alone to get used to the idea of sharing the column with him, but it was too late to back out.

Outside, he took a deep breath and felt the warmth of the sun on his face. It was only March in Phoenix, with the real scorchers at least two months away, but he wouldn't bother wearing a jacket to work much longer. He loved the golden heat of the Southwest, and the informality that came with it. Being home again filled him with a glowing inner contentment. Maybe he'd see if Amy wanted to go to a Cubs spring training baseball game.

Whoa! he nearly said out loud. Where had that idea come from? It was bad enough he had to work with a career-crazy female. He knew better than to let another workaholic get inside his head—or his bed. If Carla hadn't taught him that women obsessed with their jobs made lousy lovers, then he was too dumb to be giving anyone advice.

His new partner was walking down the street beside him, and he tried to forget the mental image of Amy's shapely legs as she sat on her desk. What he'd better *not* forget was that she definitely had a sharp cutting edge.

Had she tensed up around him in high school when he got close, or was he flattering himself? Maybe she was just stressed over sharing the column. He tried to remember her as a frizzy-haired sophomore pest, but a dozen years fogged his memory. Still, she must have made a lasting impression on him; he'd recognized her right away, even though she'd lost the curls and gained a new and improved body.

"And the beer-batter shrimp are fabulous."

"What?"

"The shrimp at Pete's Eatery—where we're going. I took your last grunt as a yes," Amy said, sounding a little miffed because he hadn't been listening.

"Oh, sounds good."

They walked under a faded green awning into a restaurant dimly lit by naked low-wattage bulbs in a tin ceiling. Pete's Eatery made a fetish out of being unpretentious. Chrome and Formica tables were crowded together between long rows of booths along the walls. Shabby beige was everywhere, and the floor had the rusty brown carpeting usually found on outdoor decks. The only good thing about it, Joe thought, was that the owner hadn't gotten cutesy by hanging junk like old eggbeaters or license plates on the walls.

"So this place is atmospheric," Joe said to make conversation as they waited for a blue-jeaned host to seat them.

"Like the room where the custodians sneaked a smoke in our old high school," Amy dryly commented.

"Funny you should mention the old school," Joe said, edging closer to her. "It's been on my mind a lot lately."

"I hardly ever give it a thought," she said offhandedly.

"This way, folks."

Joe trailed behind her as a pseudocowboy led them to a back booth. Amy quickly slipped in, picked up a menu in a scruffy maroon leather folder and studied it with an intensity most people reserved for final exams and divorce settlements.

A waitress in cutoff jeans and a frilly off-the-shoulder blouse came to take their orders. Joe opted for the super-size burger, medium rare, with double onions. If Amy thought their office was small before lunch...

"Tuna salad on whole wheat—you still make that with chopped onions and green peppers, don't you? And an order of onion rings." Amy didn't look up from the menu as she ordered.

He pursed his lips to avoid showing a grin. The battle lines were drawn, and she had no idea what tricks this veteran of the war between the sexes had in his arsenal.

"So, Joe, how did you happen to apply for this job?" She kept her nose buried in the menu. How long did it take to read through four dessert choices?

"I saw the ad in *Editor & Publisher.*"

"Oh, sure, where else?" She finally slapped the menu shut and propped it against the old-fashioned chrome napkin dispenser.

"You think maybe I have a friend on the paper?"

"No—never occurred to me." She was digging around in her bulky denim purse.

"A friend like Bug."

"Well, you picked up fast on that nickname." She came up empty-handed and tossed the purse beside her on the bench seat.

"You thought because I called him Bert—"

"No, no, I understand about the good-ol'-boy stuff—backslapping, fanny patting—"

"Cut the crap, Patterson."

She looked stunned for an instant but came back quickly.

"Did I hit a nerve?"

"No. Just because you're intimidated by the boss and I'm not—"

"Me? Intimidated? That's ridiculous!" Her voice squeaked out the protest.

"Then you must have a shoe fetish—you never once went eyeball-to-eyeball—"

"You haven't changed a bit! You always were a—"

"And I probably still am, but you weren't paying enough attention to Garver. S.Y.N.D.I.C.A.T.I.O.N."

"Don't spell at me!"

"Holly Heartfelt is a nice little local column—I'm sure it helps a lot of people work through their problems. But it doesn't have a snowball's chance in the desert of going national against biggies like—"

"A nice little column! I've never heard anything so patronizing, so, so..."

"Accurate?"

"If you don't think much of the Holly Heartfelt column, why did you take the job? Why agree to work with me?"

"Believe it or not, I didn't know about you—only that Holly was retiring and her assistant was writing the column temporarily. Remember, I already had the job, and Garver just offered it to you this morning."

Her gorgeous caramel-colored eyes took on a watery sheen, and he suddenly experienced man's most ancient terror: fear of a publicly weeping female.

"Hey, Amy, I didn't mean that as a put-down. Garver is a jerk. He should have involved you in the planning process from square one."

"Well, that's one thing we agree on."

"Be terrible for the column if we agree on too much." He was wrong about her teary eyes leading to a crying jag but not about her bruised ego.

"I suppose it would."

Their lunches came on thick platters heaped with tangled masses of curly fries. By unspoken consent, they tabled talk about the column. She brought him up-to-date on Arizona's colorful politics, and he talked about the Cubs' prospects when the regular season began. He ate so fast he could almost hear an echo from the past—his mother telling him not to wolf his food. But Amy finished ahead of him, leaving behind a heap of uneaten crusts with at least half of her sandwich attached to them.

"We'll have our checks now—separate checks, please," she told the waitress who came to ask about dessert.

"Let me..."

"No way—thanks."

2

That afternoon Joe sauntered into the tiny cubicle after a trip to the personnel office, hands stuffed into his pants pockets and shoulders hunched as though trying to make himself smaller to fit the space.

"How was your tour?" Amy asked indifferently, wishing he'd gone by way of the South Pole.

"I was suitably impressed. What are you doing?"

"Still reading last week's batch of letters."

"What's the policy on the ones you can't use?"

"Everyone gets some response. Most we send computer printouts or make a referral to an agency or expert. Some are too touchy for us to handle—medical problems, potential suicides—"

"What's the turnaround time on questions?" he interrupted.

"A week to ten days, if possible. Quicker when Holly was still working full-time."

"Too slow." He perched on the edge of his desk, nearly knocking off a stack of notebooks.

"If you think you can do it faster, here's last Thursday's pile."

She tossed a stack of unopened envelopes in the general vicinity of his lap, not caring that half of them slid down his legs to the floor before he could grab them.

"I think our first priority is to establish a system."

She could swear he'd clicked his teeth for emphasis. "I have a system. You're welcome to watch and learn."

He stood, not bothering to pick up the envelopes under his feet. "Even in the wilds of Minnesota, reporters have to do something every day to fill the space between ads. Of course, if you've never left home..."

"I worked in Prescott after college," she said stiffly, slicing open another envelope with her sharp-bladed silver letter opener. "You're standing on some questions."

He gave her a disgruntled look but bent to retrieve the scattered letters. His jacket parted at the back slit and his chinos stretched tight over a round, firm backside, easily the cutest she'd ever noticed on a tall man. She suppressed an urge to smack him where he was vulnerable and noisily shook out the next letter, trying to focus on the smeary, felt-pen words written on lined notebook paper.

"How do you handle questions from juveniles?" he asked, straightening and sorting the letters he'd gathered into an orderly pile.

"Very carefully—usually with a personal note. If they seem to have serious problems, I recommend a school counselor or refer them to a help number."

"Okay, I guess we're on the same track," he conceded.

"Well, thank you very much. Do I have your permission to go back to what I was doing?"

"What are your brothers doing these days?" he asked, ignoring her sarcasm and abruptly switching topics.

"Sonny is teaching history and coaching football in Texas. Brian is still finding himself, driving a beer truck in Tucson."

"You know, we were good friends, but I didn't know Sonny's real name until graduation. Where did your folks come up with a name like Orson Bernard Patterson?"

"My mother's brother." She wasn't in the mood for this cozy family update.

"How's your mother? I really like that lady."

"Fine—she's the merry widow of Sun City. She golfs, plays tennis." She didn't mention her mother had more dates than she did.

"Good. Now, have you cooled down enough so we can get to work—together?"

"It depends on what you mean by 'together.' I assume you'll answer your picks, and I'll work on ones I like."

"That's not quite what William III wants."

He even referred to William John Ranson III by his first name! She'd seen the publisher only twice in her four years on the paper.

"We have to pick nineties issues, especially questions on male-female relationships. Then we both answer them— that's where the his-and-her angle comes in," he explained.

"Is this the hot idea Garver hasn't told me yet?" She hadn't been this skeptical since a rip-off mechanic had tried to sell her a new transmission for her battered old car. "So do we sit around reading questions to each other?"

He shrugged, and she wasn't in the mood to play twenty questions.

"I suggest we divide all the letters on hand, screen out the impossibles, then go over the potentials together," he said.

"Brilliant plan, but I have a Holly Heartfelt column to finish first. I assume it will run until this new thing is launched."

She turned back to her computer and called up the answer to the reluctant bridesmaid. For fifteen minutes, she deleted, typed and deleted, not changing anything substantial but giving herself time to cool down.

"Good answer. I like the multiple choice."

He was standing behind her, watching as she deleted a sentence then typed it exactly as it had been. Didn't he know anything about newsroom etiquette?

"Thank you." She didn't know whether he meant it or was trying to butter her up.

They worked for a few minutes until he broke the silence. "I've found a good one. Let me read it to you."

Did she have a choice? She remembered her decrepit car, her credit card balance, the rent that was due next week...

"Go ahead."

She listened as he read an overly long, relatively dull outpouring from a woman who thought her boyfriend might be unfaithful and ready to end their relationship.

"This woman's writing a book," Amy said while he shuffled a thick sheaf of pages.

"She'd wordy, but here's the important part—'Please tell me what telltale signs to look for.'"

"I think she should confront her boyfriend," Amy said, making a mental note to ask the custodian to check out the squeak in her swivel chair. She was starting to be bothered by all kinds of things in the tiny cubicle: the faded purple pipe-cleaner elephant Holly had left behind; on the bulletin board a paper airplane she'd made herself from a Bug memo; a paper-clip chain hanging on a file cabinet handle. She'd thought of them as homey touches, but now the place seemed too crowded to put up with unnecessary clutter.

What's wrong with this scene? she asked herself. *Ah, yes, there's somebody here who seems to be using up more than his share of oxygen.*

"That's not what the writer asked," Joe observed. "She wants to know what clues to look for."

"How to tell if a relationship is over," Amy mused, getting interested in the question in spite of her unhappiness over working with her old nemesis. "Easy. When the boyfriend takes his toothbrush and razor home with him the morning after."

"After what?" he asked with feigned innocence.

"After you-know-what."

"I didn't expect euphemisms from a woman of the nineties like you."

"You didn't expect me, period."

"Getting back to the question," he said dryly, "why don't we slant it to help both sexes. A man can tell the relationship is over when she starts using his toothbrush to clean the grout around the shower tiles."

"Yuck! Did you dredge that up from personal experience?"

"No, but feel free to share your innermost secrets for the good of the column."

"I'll stick to the hypothetical. What if the boyfriend calls out an ex-lover's name while in the throes of passion?"

"What if he doesn't call at all?" he suggested.

"If he sticks little foil-wrapped packets in his suitcase for a business trip she's not going on?"

"That's a cruel one. Were you snooping when you found them?"

"Why do you think it happened to me?" Hot cheeks were giving her away again!

"Just a hunch. Or maybe I'm a mind reader."

"Ha! For your information, I was tucking a note in his carryon, but that was ages ago, and it was the best thing that could have happened. He used to be on the *Monitor* staff, and I learned never, ever to date a man I have to work with."

She'd long since gotten over her feelings for that slimeball, but she would never forget how embarrassing it was to see an ex-lover at work, day after day, week after week, a living reminder of how dumb it was to be intimate with a co-worker.

"Seeing anyone special now?" Joe asked in a casual tone that emphasized her answer was of no real consequence to him.

"Not special as in madly in love." A tremendous understatement.

"If you ever need coaching from the male point of view..."

"That day will never come!"

"I'll let the offer stand just in case. It's time we knocked off for the day. I'm sharper in the morning."

"You going home already? I'm only just warming up," she said blithely, inwardly cheering his early departure but unable to resist a barb. "Someone might think your mother has dinner on the table for you."

"No, my parents retired to Sedona, but I believe in taking off when quitting time comes around. I'm no workaholic."

Now she knew he hadn't moved back with his parents—not that it mattered in the least to her whether he lived alone or with someone.

"Well, I wasted too much time today. I need to stay here and catch up," she said.

"No hot date tonight?"

"You're awfully interested in my love life. Ever think of working for the *National Insider?*" she asked.

"Just checking out your credentials. I wouldn't expect you to write about sports if you don't know a tight end from the end zone."

"Spoken with true Western chauvinism."

"That's my exit cue. I'd rather ride one of those old mechanical bulls than debate feminist issues. See you tomorrow."

She watched him go, not realizing she was biting her lower lip until it started to hurt.

It was 5:01 when Joe moved out of her range of vision. She slumped back in her chair and stared up at the ceiling—the newsroom ceiling. The cubicle was like an aquarium, with glass walls on three sides and no top. She felt like a goldfish sharing space with a giant squid.

At least now she knew he was a morning person. Her best working time was evening, when the newsroom was relatively deserted. She could accomplish more in the quiet hour after five than in a full morning with constant interruptions.

As long as she had any say, Holly Heartfelt's column wouldn't be replaced by a humor piece. Scrubbing grout with a toothbrush! Many of the people who wrote had real problems; they were hurting and needed moral support as well as practical suggestions.

She grabbed a stack of envelopes and started scanning letters, determined to weed out any that invited flip answers.

An hour and a half later, she had a stack of rejects, several heartrending letters calling for serious answers, and two very iffy nineties-type questions.

Lunch was only a bad memory, and she was starved. She was headed toward the vending machines when she remembered it—the date. She was supposed to meet a graduate student from ASU at a coffee bar near the campus. Espresso with Ed. The thought was depressing. He was cute enough—except for a receding hairline and the little potbelly he tried to conceal by never tucking in his shirt—but she didn't feel up to another lecture on the molecular structure of some single-celled something or other. Tonight was going to be their last date.

"I hate dating," she told the soda machine, feeding in her quarters to get a diet cola.

She moved on to the sandwich machine, studied the offerings and used up the rest of her coins on a ham and cheese.

When she got back to her desk, she had messages. Her mother wanted to know if she'd gotten the job, but it was no use calling her back because she had a date.

"Have fun, Mom," Amy said to the machine, glad Melanie wasn't there to hear her conversations with mechanical friends.

"Amy, this is Ed," the machine played for her. "I'm too involved in my research to meet you tonight. Keep in touch."

She had a pretty good idea whom he was researching: a fellow graduate student with blunt-cut black hair, a big nose and a chest that invited speculation about silicone implants. She'd stopped by the table on their last date and talked science stuff until Amy had nearly fallen asleep.

Darn! She really hated letting a protozoa like Ed think he'd dumped her. Her timing was lousy. She should have canceled the date herself. Forget sparing any man's feelings!

She started reading a lackluster letter from a woman feuding with her sister over their deceased mother's keepsake three-carat diamond.

"Sell it and divide the money, you greedy vultures," she muttered, flicking the question onto the reject pile. That one would get a computer printout on the equitable division of estates.

"Still working?"

She was so startled she stood and knocked over her chair.

"Sorry, I didn't mean to scare you." Joe was standing in the doorway, hands thrust into the pockets of jeans this time.

"I didn't expect you to come back," she said, righting her chair before he had a chance to play Sir Galahad. "But since you're here, you can take a look at this letter. It's from a guy who says his girlfriend insists her Doberman share the bed with them. Nineties enough for you?"

"What is it with pet lovers who want hair balls in their beds?" he asked facetiously. "I'll think about it in the morning. I only came back because I have a couple of ideas for the format."

"I thought you don't work nights."

"I don't want to hang around here. Thought maybe you could pry yourself from that chair and come with me—"

"Stop there. I don't date the men I work with—no exceptions."

"Who said anything about a date? You're interested in launching the new column as soon as possible, aren't you?"

"I'm the one working overtime," she reminded him, embarrassed because she'd mistakenly interpreted his invitation as a personal thing.

"If you have other plans for the evening . . ."

"No, I don't, but we can talk here."

"Not tonight. The Suns are in town, and an old buddy gave me two tickets he can't use. I thought we could go to the game and talk business during the time-outs. Unless you're one of those women who can't stand basketball."

"Talk during the game?" she asked suspiciously. "Doesn't sound like a business meeting to me."

"What part sounds like a date?"

"Going in your car, using your ticket, sitting beside you . . ."

"You can drive instead of me, or follow me in your car. Pay for the ticket if you like, but I got it free. As for sitting beside me, it will be pretty hard to talk if you don't."

"All right, I'll meet you there. Give me one of the tickets."

"I was hoping you'd drive. I have a hole in my muffler. Hate to get a ticket my first night back in town."

"Oh, all right, but don't blame me if you're embarrassed riding in my old car."

"It takes more than that to embarrass me."

* * *

The game looked like a sellout when they got there, and already the lines at the refreshment stands were six deep.

"Hungry?" he asked. "I haven't had dinner."

"Neither have I." She thought of her abandoned vending-machine sandwich without regrets.

"Since we're not on a date and I got the tickets, you probably want to buy me a chili dog," he suggested.

"Sounds fair."

"Thanks. I'll have a large order of nachos with it, and a jumbo pop. Hot stuff makes me thirsty."

"Any special kind?" she asked, annoyed.

"Surprise me. You don't mind if I go to my seat, do you? I don't want to miss the beginning of the game by standing in line. You did come along just to talk business."

"I'll get your order." She stepped to the end of a long line and muttered under her breath, "I'll get you, too!"

"Thanks, Patterson." He was already walking away, but he turned and yelled back, "This isn't the way I treat my dates!"

Their seats were just below cloud level, and the pressed-cardboard carrying tray was in danger of collapsing at any moment. She had to climb over only half a dozen pairs of size fourteen feet to get to him, and by then her hand was sticky with spilled cola.

"Thanks, Patterson."

He watched the game like an air-traffic controller juggling half a hundred jets, but true to his word, he did talk shop during time-outs and between periods.

"We need a catchy name. 'His and Hers' sounds like monogrammed towels," he said.

"I always thought the paper would continue the Holly Heartfelt name."

He grimaced at her but didn't respond.

"I admit it sounds old-fashioned," she said, "but it has a homey, reliable ring."

"Like an old flannel robe worn through at the elbows," he said dryly.

The teams returned before they could settle on a name they both liked, and the second half of the game was exciting enough to keep her attention riveted on the court. The Suns were playing the Lakers, and the lead changed so often there wasn't time to say a word without missing something. By the time the home team won it, she'd almost forgotten why she was there.

"You watched the game," he said on the way out. "That's a sure sign I wasn't with a date."

"You only go out with women who hate sports?"

"Not intentionally, but it seems to work out that way. I'm grateful if my date even pretends to be interested."

"Doesn't say much for your taste in women," she snorted.

They slowly worked their way through the exuberant crowd and returned to her car.

"What a traffic jam! I hate tie-ups like this," she said.

He pushed back the rolled cuffs on his black denim shirt and smiled, but he didn't offer to drive through the tangle of vehicles trying to get away.

"That chili gave me a raging thirst," he said. "I'll buy you a drink to pay you back for the snacks—if it's not too datelike."

"We haven't settled on a name for the column yet. I suppose it would take more than one drink to turn this into a date."

"Not dating is more complicated than dating," he teased. "You have to make up the rules as you go along." He gave her directions to a little sports bar near the *Monitor* parking lot where he'd left his car.

He ordered near beer, and she had a fuzzy navel, relishing every sip of the thirst-quenching peachy drink.

"So, are you glad to be home?" she asked, not really in the mood for more talk about the column.

"Sure am. I got tired of snow, and Minnesota mosquitoes are meaner than our Arizona scorpions and almost as big. Besides, where else can I see baseball and basketball in March?"

She wondered about more personal things but didn't ask. One drink had given her a sense of relaxed well-being, and she didn't want the evening to get complicated. She waited while he finished another nonalcoholic beer, then drove him back to his car.

"Thanks, Patterson. See you tomorrow," he said matter-of-factly as he got out of her car.

She drove home slowly, feeling as though she'd just eaten a giant sour pickle. Something about the evening wasn't right, but she couldn't put her finger on it.

At home, she parked her dusty compact car in her reserved spot and climbed the outer stairs to her second-floor apartment, still wondering why she felt so unsettled. It wasn't because she had to share the column. Nothing about that arrangement puzzled her—she was just plain mad about that. Something else was nagging at her.

Her apartment was blessedly quiet. Was the neighbor's stereo out of order? She kicked off her heels and padded across the desert tan carpeting to her bedroom, more than ready to fall into bed.

On the nightstand, the red light was blinking on the answering machine, but she wanted to think about the evening for a few minutes before she tackled her messages.

She slipped out of her once-crisp suit, gave the wrinkles a dour look and bundled it up for the cleaners. She'd been overdressed for a basketball game, but it hadn't mattered. She'd had fun anyway.

That was it! She'd actually enjoyed her non-date with Malone. What was her life coming to when she had more fun on a business meeting with an unwanted partner than with any real date in recent memory?

"Great," she said, indulging in gloom while she peeled off her panty hose.

She was in a lousy mood to start with, so nothing on her answering machine could ruin the rest of the evening. She sat on the edge of the bed and pushed the playback button.

She listened absentmindedly to her mother's message. "So if you're trying to call me and I'm not here, it's because Larry asked me to go to Vegas for a few days. But I do hope you got the column job, Amy. No, I don't hope—I'm sure you did! I have confidence in you. I'll call when I get back. Bye-bye, honey."

Larry. Was he the silver fox with the gold tooth? Her mother was enjoying the rush of attention she'd gotten since joining the tennis club, and Amy was happy for her. Also, selfishly speaking, it was much easier to be best friends with a mother who was too busy to monitor her daughter's every move.

The next message got her full attention.

"Patterson, this is Bertram Garver. We need some publicity shots for the column. Wear something sharp tomorrow."

His message was a puzzler. What did he consider sharp? She didn't own a navy pin-striped suit or an old school tie, and she wasn't about to be photographed in her black gabardine suit with the boxy jacket—suitable for job interviews and funerals.

She rifled through her closet, remembering the days when she and her best friend, Tina, had spent hours on the phone every evening deciding what to wear to school the next day. Not that it mattered; in those days she looked lumpy in anything she wore.

Not anymore, she thought gratefully, sliding shut the closet door, but what on earth did Bug expect her to be wearing tomorrow? She thought of talking to someone about it, but the first person who came to mind was Joe. As if she'd call him to chat about clothes!

"Like it or not, Bug," she said to her answering machine, "I'll wear whatever suits my mood."

When the alarm rang the next morning, she woke up irritated, remembering Garver's huge betrayal. How many times had he encouraged her to do the work of two by dangling the job of head columnist in front of her?

At least she could look forward to seeing her contract. Garver had hinted at a raise, and did she ever need the extra money! Her last roommate, Marcella, a Home Shopping Network addict, had moved in with a boyfriend, sticking Amy with full rent on the lease. Living there was a financial burden, but finding a good roommate was almost as difficult as succeeding in the dating game. Soul mates, male or female, were in short supply in her circle of acquaintances.

For once, her hair dried into a perfect bob after her shower, so all she had to worry about was deciding on an outfit to meet Garver's idea of "sharp."

Too bad there wasn't a pesticide to repel that Bug, she thought, then groaned at her own corniness.

"I can't believe I write for a living," she told her hair dryer.

Forget Garver! How did she want to look in a photograph? What she needed was a neckline that would flatter her. She pulled out a jade knit dress, shook her head and put it on anyway. It was too short and clingy for office wear, but she loved the scoop neck.

When she got to the office, she was curious to see what Joe was wearing. He strolled in, hands in his pockets as usual. What was that man protecting in there?

He was wearing a deep blue denim work shirt, tan slacks and a red tie with tiny figures that turned out to be cartoon characters when he got close enough for her to see them.

"Did you get a call from Garver last night?" she asked.

"Yup."

"And that's the look you chose to promote the column?" She had to admit to herself that he looked good—but not like a serious giver of advice.

Joe went through the motions of settling down to work, but when Amy suggested coffee, he volunteered to get it. If there was one thing he'd learned working with female co-workers at his previous job, they were touchy about who fetched the brew.

He'd thought a lot last night about how to approach this job, but only one conclusion stuck in his mind: Stay cool. He remembered his experiences with Amy on the school paper and knew she went in for drastic measures, like boycotting the chess tournament because no girls were in the chess club. Now there had been a hot issue! What the hell had he gotten himself into? He hoped returning to his home turf was worth the hassle of trying to work with the little fireball. He could only hope her personality had improved as much as her body! He had no complaints on that score, except she was a distraction when a man wanted to work, especially this morning. What had Garver said to inspire her to wear that dress? Not that he was complaining!

He took his time getting the coffee, talking with a few people by the coffee machine. When he got back, she had her nose buried in a letter; she was chewing on the end of a pencil as she read.

"I see you're a pencil biter," he said, setting her steaming mug on a stack of papers on her cluttered desk.

"I imagine we both have little habits that will irritate the other one," she said frostily.

"Did I sound irritated? My apologies. I don't care what you nibble. Here, try this. I've heard it's tasty, although I myself don't indulge." He handed her a leather-covered appointment book but softened his teasing with a chuckle.

"You've made your point. You won't come in and find me gnawing at the padding on your chair."

"We partners should work out these little differences with good, honest communication," he said. "I, of course, have no bad habits."

She looked pointedly at his hands. "Bet you rip out a lot of pants pockets."

"Now you're getting personal."

He felt like the heavy in a passé old movie when she flushed becomingly, but teasing her was fun. He firmly believed in having a good time, especially at work.

"Hi, you two." Roberta poked her head into their cubicle. "How was your date, Amy?"

"A strikeout."

"Amy, I thought we weren't on a date," he said.

"Am I missing something?" Roberta asked.

"I'll explain later why I didn't have a date last night," Amy said.

Apparently, Roberta picked up on some girl-type signal. She faded away into the newsroom.

"Am I the strikeout?" Joe asked.

"No, you weren't even in the ball game," Amy said crossly.

"So someone stood you up. Sorry about that. I meant it when I offered to give you advice from a man's point of view."

"Stuff it, Joe. I'd rather take advice from Louie, the mail clerk."

"You're not a morning person, are you?"

"Emphatically no."

"Can you give me a ballpark figure on the time when I should start talking to you?"

"Five p.m."

"I wasn't expecting a silent partnership. Should we pass notes? Or we could get a chalkboard."

"Oh, stop it, Joe. I know how you can needle people."

"Is that what I did when I was your high school editor—needle you?" Surprising as it was, she'd actually hurt his feelings. "I thought I was a regular guy, firm but fair."

"Oh, sure, your friends got to cover student government, newsbreaks, hot issues. I got the chess club and band tournaments. You punished me for a year because I nearly beat you out for the editor's job."

"Sophomores never got to be editor. You had to learn your place. It was nothing personal."

"Well, I took it personally!"

"I can't believe you remember all that stuff. It's been years!"

"At least a dozen—and it's not in the least important now."

"Good." He smiled but didn't believe her. "Let's see those two letters you think are possibilities for our first column."

An hour later, he was sure of one thing. She was a hard worker. Nothing got past her, and her idea of a break was taking a sip of cold coffee. It was a relief when the photographer called up that he was ready to take their publicity shots.

Somewhat to Joe's surprise, Bert Garver was in the small studio when he and Amy got there.

"This is Paul Lambeau, our best photographer," Garver said with phony heartiness. "Wait till you see his work on a billboard."

"On a what?" Amy asked.

"We're launching your column on billboards all over metropolitan Phoenix. I don't need to tell you how much is riding on making a splash locally. Good dress choice, Amy."

"You mean this picture will be on billboards?"

"You won't be able to drive a mile without seeing one," Garver said proudly.

"You do mean a head-and-shoulder shot, don't you?" She sounded on the verge of panic.

"Oh, no. Full figure."

"Joe, did you know this?"

"I had an inkling."

"And you didn't tell me?"

"I assumed you knew." He wasn't sure whether to feel guilty or laugh at her reaction.

"Mr. Garver, there's been a remake of *Attack of the 50 Ft. Woman.* I'm not about to star in the Phoenix version," she argued.

"It's for the good of the column," Garver said sanctimoniously. "And naturally I expect your full cooperation, if you intend to sign the contract you'll be getting this afternoon."

Joe didn't feel good about the way Garver turned the screws, but he wasn't self-destructive enough to fight a great promotional idea. If the column didn't fly, they'd both be out on the street. He could probably get his old job back—in the cold, snowy Midwest.

"We'll try this two ways and see which works," the photographer said, indifferent to anything he couldn't focus on through his lens. "First, I want to shoot you separately. Show me some antagonism. Amy, you're ready to throttle this guy for his macho viewpoints. Give me anger."

"That's easy!"

The session began.

If there was anything more tedious than being a model, Joe didn't know what it was. When his turn to pose finally came, he thought the boredom would put him to sleep before the guy finished fooling with his camera and started snapping.

Garver came and went during the session, too self-important to trust his brainchild with a mere top-notch photographer.

"Now for something friendlier," Paul said, changing the backdrop for the next series of poses. "This time I want you to pretend you like each other."

"You should have hired actors," Amy grumbled.

These poses went even more slowly. When Joe had to drape his arm around Amy, her shoulders were as stiff as a board.

"This isn't flying," the photographer complained. "Hey, people, you're a team. You're posing like Abe Lincoln and the Missus. Be natural. This is supposed to be fun, remember? Give me some animation."

Just then, Garver made another foray into the studio, staying by the door as though he were a casual observer.

"Mr. Garver, this is the dumbest—" Amy began.

Maybe she wanted to commit career suicide, but Joe wasn't going to fall on the sword with her. He grabbed her and silenced her in the only way he could think of. He covered her mouth with his.

"Great idea!" the photographer crooned. "Keep it going, kids. Yeah, yeah."

Joe took her in his arms, thwarting her escape attempt, and emphatically kissed her, moving his lips against hers to the steady click-click of the camera and clucks of approval from Garver.

"Do it again—yes!" Paul urged.

To Joe's surprise, she was hardly fighting him at all now.

After a final token resistance, she went limp in his arms. Even more surprising, he didn't care anymore how long the shoot took. There were many worse ways to spend the morning.

"That's a wrap. You two can stop now—if you want to," the man behind the camera joked.

Joe let go of her, bracing himself for a hurricane-force outburst of protest. Instead, she rubbed her mouth with the back of her hand and stared at him speechlessly.

He took advantage of the lull before the storm and hurried over to say a few words to Garver, managing to steer him into the corridor and out of earshot before Amy reacted.

He felt like a man who'd just ridden a tiger and couldn't wait to try again once he was sure his limbs were all intact. After Garver left him, he shook his head to come out of his daze and beat a hasty retreat. Amy Patterson had a honey-sweet mouth and a body to inspire erotic dreams, but she was as career hungry as any woman he'd met, exactly the kind of woman he'd sworn to avoid after he and Carla broke it off. If Patterson ever wore a dress like that to work again, he'd send her home to change. Or find himself a closet where he could get some work done.

"Damn it, women make life so complicated," he muttered under his breath as he escaped.

3

Amy felt branded. Hurrying through the newsroom, she was sure her lips were swollen and the skin around them a telltale pink. Joe must have kissed away every last trace of her "guaranteed to last all day" lipstick.

She retrieved her purse from the file, where she kept it under *N* for necessity, then squatted down beside the metal cabinet to repair her makeup using the tiny rectangular mirror clamped to her lipstick tube. Here and under the desk were the only blind spots in her fishbowl office.

"So he's a great kisser," she mumbled to the black plastic lipstick case. "What's a kiss? Only a pucker with suction."

She stood and yanked on her dress, trying to coax it down over her thighs, but the extra inch she gained made her bra show at the neckline.

"Time for my emergency sweater," she said aloud, re-filing her purse under *N* and digging into the *S* file. "Work—yes, work. Important to be working when he gets here."

She scrambled to her terminal and called up a letter she'd been writing to a friend in California, determined to look busy when he returned to the office even if her concentration was nil. She wasn't in any condition to be giving advice! Not that she hadn't suspected Joe would be a good kisser. He probably excelled at all kinds of erotic arts.

She could imagine those warm, flexible lips parting hers while his hands roamed over...

"Enough of that!" she ordered herself, furtively glancing around to see if anyone had witnessed her irrational behavior.

Her reaction to Joe's kisses just proved it had been too long since she'd been kissed by someone who knew how. She certainly didn't have the hots for Joe Malone! Even if he was—well, sexy—she would never, ever get involved with a co-worker again.

"It's just been too long," she firmly asserted to her computer, saving the letter to her friend for another day.

"Talking to yourself?" Joe asked, coming up behind her so quietly he made her jump. "Hey, my grandmother has a sweater like that."

"It's my mother's," she said, not telling him she'd found the pale pink synthetic knit in her mother's Goodwill bag. "I keep it here for when the air-conditioning is set too cold." He was making her feel like an elderly lady in a smock and hair net. "We'd better get to work. What do you think about the cat question?"

"Hmm." He plopped down at the other screen.

The two desks were arranged in an L, which worked well as long as they both didn't push back their chairs at the same instant. It also meant she was free of Joe's scrutiny as long as he worked at the computer.

"Here it is," she said, reading aloud a portion of the letter. "'I'm allergic to cats. My girlfriend has two and just took in a stray she wants to keep. What should I do?'"

"I remember that one," Joe said.

"The solution is easy. He should get allergy shots."

"I vote for a new girlfriend." He leaned back in the swivel chair and glanced over at her screen.

"That's pretty drastic." She suppressed an urge to shield her screen with her arms.

"She knows the poor guy's allergic. I see the third cat as a sign the relationship is nearly over anyway. We've already worked on telltale signs. I'll let you make the call on whether we use this one."

"Put it on hold. In case we get caught short sometime."

"I'll let you send out an answer," he said.

"Have you noticed that you 'let' me do things when you don't want to do them?" she asked.

"It's no big deal. I can crank out a letter if you want me to."

"That's not my point, Joe. I'll be glad to do it—just ask. 'Let' sounds like you're giving me permission or doing me a favor. It's condescending."

"So we're back to the big issue—who's running the column."

"I was only pointing out one of your little quirks." She made her back ramrod straight and stared at her screen.

"I've picked up on a few of yours, too."

"Like what?" She swiveled around to stare at him.

"Not eating your crusts."

"Crusts! What do they have to do with writing a column?"

"Most women eat half a sandwich and take the other half home instead of building a pyramid out of the crusts."

She made a scoffing noise meant to imply this argument was beneath her. "Do you know anything I don't about Garver's new idea for the column?"

"You're changing the subject, but no, I don't. Let's get back to the questions. Here's one. 'I just moved to town, and I hate the bar scene. How can I meet women?'"

"Women are everywhere. Meeting a nice man is much tougher."

"Only if you make up cockeyed rules. What's wrong with meeting a guy where you work? Simple, natural, and you start with something in common."

"Oh, sure, and when it's over you see his smug face for days and weeks and months. You can't forget the jerk because he's always around."

"I'll concede—it could take a sticky turn, but it wouldn't happen very often."

"Not to you. Women never dump you, so you never have to dread elevator encounters or cold stares at the drinking fountain."

"You make it sound like you're an authority on my love life. If you're curious—"

"Certainly not!"

"My last breakup was mutual. She had a chance to advance her career by going to New York. It just happened."

"You're not going to tell me there were no telltale signs of crumbling coupledom, no little irritations that paved the way?"

"I suppose her fourteen-hour days were a pretty good clue. Now, can we get back to important things, like writing a column?"

"Sure, but—" She was interrupted by a buzz from their phone.

He mumbled into the receiver, then got up to go. "Good news. I'm getting a legal parking spot. Be back as soon as I can."

The purple pipe-cleaner elephant leered at her with pink sequin eyes, and she decided to use the breathing spell to dispose of all the cutesy junk—some hers and some left by Holly—that cluttered the tiny cubicle. Maybe Joe would take her more seriously if she got rid of her soup-can pencil holder and her collection of Christmas-party gag gifts. She was deciding whether to toss a pinecone turkey into the wastebasket when Louie, the morose kid who worked in the mailroom, brought two manila envelopes.

"This one's yours," he said in his funeral-parlor voice. "The new guy gets the other one."

"Thanks, Louie. Hear any good jokes today?"

"Naw." He was the only male on the premises who could be relied upon not to have one. He dropped Joe's envelope beside his terminal and left.

She was almost afraid to open hers. What if Bug's idea of a good raise was hiking her pay ten cents an hour? Was it worth the aggravation of working with her old nemesis if she didn't get a fair salary increase?

Her envelope wasn't sealed, only held shut by little metal tabs that went through a hole in the flap. She opened it and pulled out a sheaf of pages, scanning paragraph after paragraph of single-spaced legal jargon until she came to the clincher.

"Yes, yes, yes!" She couldn't rush down to order a Mercedes, but she wouldn't have to risk a classified-ad roommate.

Going over all the fine print would put her to sleep, so she filed the envelope with her purse. Might as well save it for bedtime reading. She only had one question: How much were they paying Joe to work on her column?

His envelope, pristine except for his name printed on the front, was so close she could reach it with one casual swivel.

Maybe I should test this chair before I ask for oiling, she thought, propelling it around the small floor space, coincidentally coming to a stop right beside Joe's desk.

Of course, she wouldn't dream of opening his envelope, but maybe if she really concentrated—well, a lot of people claimed to get psychic messages by holding significant objects.

The businesslike tan envelope was completely opaque. She confirmed it by holding it against the bulb in her desk lamp.

"Open it, if you're that curious."

"*Eek!*" Her guilty shriek was almost as embarrassing as being caught with his contract. "I haven't read it!"

She stood, dropped the envelope beside his terminal and backed against the edge of her desk. Blood rushed to her cheeks, and she knew how captured felons felt.

"You need a collar with a bell so you can't sneak up on people," she said.

It was a weak joke, and he wasn't amused. He advanced closer, until her bottom was wedged uncomfortably against the hard metal desk. She couldn't retreat from that broad, muscular chest.

"You can't wriggle out of this by clouding the issue with your kinky fantasy," he warned.

She couldn't think of a comeback, not with his aftershave teasing her nostrils and his strong, smooth chin jutting so close to her face.

"You're an inveterate snoop, Patterson. You need a self-help group for compulsive meddlers."

"You're just as bad—always sneaking up on me. You think you're the editor and I'm the peon on this column."

"Is that your excuse for reading my personal mail?"

"I didn't read it."

"Well, go ahead." He casually moved away as though intimidating her had been the last thing on his mind.

"No, I never intended—"

"Read it, Amy." Every word oozed threat.

"This is ridic—"

"Read!"

What could he do if she refused? A really bizarre image flitted through her mind, and it took a moment to realize her bottom was smarting only because the desk edge was so hard.

Quickly, before she lost her last iota of nerve, she removed his contract from the envelope and flipped to the crucial paragraph.

"We're being paid the same."

"Did you expect to get more?"

"I have more seniority on the paper," she said half-heartedly, relieved that at least her salary wasn't lower than his.

"I'm going to lunch."

Five minutes after he left, she regained enough presence of mind to blame the old pink sweater for making the office feel like a sauna.

By the time he got to the street, Joe was grinning. The little sneak! The hardest part of this job was not trampling on her bruised ego. He was sympathetic. She'd expected to be handed the column and instead she got him. But when he'd seen her with his contract, he'd been mad enough to... what? Anything she deserved was definitely politically incorrect!

Did he think he was James Cagney mashing a grapefruit in his moll's face in an old movie?

As he race-walked over the hot pavement, his smile only got broader. Wild-haired Amy had rearranged herself into all those sleek lines and luscious curves, but underneath her new, improved exterior, she was still the same old firebrand, tilting at windmills without realizing what a dynamite woman she was. But like so many women obsessed with causes, she was wearing blinders that kept her from seeing her pathway to success for what it really was—a lonely treadmill.

He sighed with relief. Kissing her had confused him for a brief time, but he wouldn't let himself be dazzled by her charms. He'd sworn off workaholic career women, no matter how cute.

By the time he reached a hole-in-the-wall Mexican restaurant, his saner self was back in control. If they could channel the antagonism between them into the column, they both might be on to a good thing.

When he finished his authentically spicy lunch, he returned to the office to find her slaving over the computer. "Didn't you go out for lunch?" He tried to sound nonchalantly nonpatronizing but friendly.

"No time. I've made a list of seventeen places to meet singles," she said.

He took up the challenge, and half an hour later his own list was almost as long as hers. "I started with health clubs," he said.

"They're okay if you're into group sweating. My first choice was service clubs."

"Lunch with potbellied married men? There's a hot possibility."

"Maybe we should skip the editorializing," she suggested.

"Okay, how about a pool league?"

"Swimming?"

"No, pool as in eight ball."

"Okay, it has possibilities," she admitted. "I put shopping next. Sometimes supermarkets have special evenings for singles."

The phone buzzed, and Joe picked it up.

"We've been summoned," he said after a few terse responses to the caller.

"Let me guess. Bug wants us to scurry up there."

The boss made Amy nervous, but Joe suspected that anything he did to calm her down would only light her fuse.

Garver stood when they came into his office. "How's it going, boys and girls?"

"Fine, sir," Amy said in her soft, placate-the-boss voice. She seemed fascinated by his cordovan wing tips.

"Have a seat. I want to run my new idea past you. I talked the publisher into a special series—the kind of pieces that could lead to syndication in the Sunday supplements. You can follow the question-and-answer format in your five weekday columns, but Sunday has to be a real attention-getter. How's this sound to you? Dating Etiquette in the Nineties.''

"Dating etiquette?" Joe nodded and pursed his lips, hoping he looked contemplative.

"You mean things like opening doors, using the right forks?" Amy asked.

"Absolutely not! I don't want anything you can get in a book. I'm talking about fieldwork, relating to the readers' problems through firsthand experiences. You two are going to start dating!''

"But—but I'm not seeing anyone regularly," Amy stammered.

"You are now—until this series is wrapped up." He pointed his finger at Joe.

"Oh, no!" Blood rushed to her face, and her cheeks positively glowed. "I didn't read anything like this in the contract.''

"It says you'll do all research prudent and essential to your assignments. This is an assignment. Get out on the street and personally find out what's happening on the dating scene. Then tell your readers how to avoid pitfalls by doing things the right way.''

"We were just working on a list of ways to meet singles," Amy said. "If we operate separately, we can cover a lot more territory.''

"Your readers don't want a rehash of the current events calendar. They want nitty-gritty details—the juicier, the better. I'll be expecting your first piece to run a week from Sunday.'' The conference was over.

Joe followed her onto the elevator, and together they rode down, the silence between them broken only by the angry staccato of her heels on the tiles of the newsroom floor.

"I'm going to get a soda," she said.

"Get me one, too, would you?"

He pulled his hand out of his pocket with some change, but before he could give it to her, she'd charged off to the left toward the vending machines.

He stood a moment, watching the bouncy motion of her bottom as she hurried across the room, dodging desks and less energetic co-workers. The way a woman walked got to him quicker than anything. Just his bad luck to have a partner with out-of-bounds signs posted on her sexy rear.

He sauntered off to their cubicle, beginning to realize what a pain "dating" Amy might become. It had been too long since he'd done anything about man's basic urge—his irrational response to Patterson was proof of that. He needed to put his bad experience with Carla behind him, but he never again wanted to get physical with a woman who was figuring out work assignments when she was between the sheets with him.

Where to Meet People of the Opposite Sex. He reread the title of his list but couldn't think of any clever meeting places. Hell, what was wrong with taking the easy way— meeting at work? A paper this big had a virtual army of eager interns and helpful office staffers to choose from.

"Catch!"

He was startled by the soda can she tossed at him. He grabbed the cold, wet missile, then eyed her suspiciously but didn't open it.

"I pull the tab and it fizzes all over me, right? I think I have the right change to pay you." He set the can aside to let it settle and dug into his pants pocket.

"My treat. Or maybe I should put it on my expense account now that we're 'dating.'"

"Didn't think of that fringe benefit. Maybe we should let the *Monitor* buy our lunches."

"You were in on this, weren't you?"

"In on what?" He tried for a bland, disinterested tone, but the corner of his mouth twitched upward in a half grin.

"Dating etiquette! What he really wants is The Sex Life of Singles."

"He wants to sell papers. That's his job," he mildly reminded her.

"You are behind this!"

"We tossed around some ideas during my interview, but nothing was firmed up. I didn't even know you worked here. If I'd known my new partner was the office version of a couch potato, I never would have suggested field research."

He enjoyed the way her lower lip quivered into a faint suggestion of a pout.

"I'm basking in your good opinion of me," she said stiffly.

"Let me ask you this," he said. "What's the worst date you've ever been on?"

"Why do you want to know?"

"Look at it this way. We'll be going out because we have a series to write. We're not expecting to have fun, so whatever happens, it won't be a disappointment. Whereas on a real date, you anticipate a good time—"

"I get it. I get it."

"So what was your worst?"

"Easy. In college, a guy who worked on the campus paper asked me to a movie. He said casual, so I wore jeans and a T-shirt. He wasn't sure I was dressed well enough to sit on his lamb's-fleece seat covers."

"He had a fancy car?"

"No, a decrepit old truck. He took me to one of those movies where heads explode and intestines spill out. Then afterward, he tried to convert me to some wacky religion. He was the only practicing member west of the Mississippi, and he needed regular sex to rekindle his inner light."

Joe laughed and stretched lazily.

"Now your turn—if you've ever had a bad date," she said.

"Why wouldn't I? Just because I'm a guy?"

"Because you're so...well, never mind."

"So what?"

"Confident?" she lamely suggested.

"I met my nightmare date when I was a freshman. She was a sophomore, an older woman. I thought she was something special until she brought her roommate on our first date."

"Maybe she was shy."

"Her roommate was male. A platonic friend, but they slept together because she was helping him get in touch with his 'artistic core.' She did offer to exorcise my inner demons by having sex with me, too."

"Scary woman. Did you take her up on it?"

"I was telling you about my worst date, remember?" He opened his can of soda and took a long swig. "Still not the right temperature for you in here?"

"Oh, no, it's fine."

"I thought you might be too hot now. Your cheeks are bright pink."

"Oh, well, maybe it is a little warm."

"Or maybe hearing the S.E.X. word makes you uncomfortable."

"Of course not! That's ridiculous!"

"You know, we're going to touch on some intimate issues—the first kiss, who pays for the date, what to do if you get a lacy black garter belt for Valentine's Day."

"How do you ever get your work done? We've got questions to answer, a series to write," she said, eager to change the subject.

"A first date to plan."

"We can count the basketball game," she said.

"Too easy. We have to experience the what-to-wear jitters, the what-to-say sweaty palms, all the insecurities—"

"You mean go through the whole dumb ritual? Where are you from? Are you into skydiving? Have you ever had a mole removed?"

"We have to have something to write about. How do you meet the men you date?"

"Through friends, in the laundry room of my apartment complex, the usual ways."

"Too dull. Let's pretend we meet in a dark, smoky club. You're sitting alone at the bar—"

"No way!"

"Don't interrupt. This is my fantasy. I sidle up to you—"

"Sidle?"

"You'll be wearing something indescribably sexy under your bulky trench coat—leave the pink sweater home."

"I'm wearing a trench coat at this time of year in Phoenix?"

"Okay, I'm flexible. I'll wear the trench coat. You wear a short leather skirt—very short, with one of those stretchy things that looks like the top of a sock."

"End of fantasy!" At least she was laughing.

"I was just warming up." In fact, he was a little too warm. He cleared his throat and tried to focus on the problem at hand. "But if you insist, I'll come over and help you do your laundry."

"Be practical."

"Maybe you could put an ad in the personals, and I could answer it. Give the classifieds a plug. Or we could sign up for a video dating service."

She was chewing the end of her pencil, probably not a sign that she liked these ideas.

"I guess those things take too long," he admitted before she could raise objections.

"Etiquette is such a formal word," she said thoughtfully.

"For once we agree. I'd rather think of it as the pitfalls and pratfalls of fraternizing with the opposite sex."

"How about this scenario? We go to a basketball game with other dates. I'm carrying one of those flimsy trays loaded with food and drinks...."

"What kind of cad would let you fetch the refreshments?"

"Good point," she said dryly. "You didn't let me get to the good part where we collide and you get soaked with icy cola."

"It's past my prime time, and I like to quit early on Fridays. Matter of principle. Let's table this and go at it again on Monday."

"Fine," she said in the snippy voice women use when they mean just the opposite. "I have a lot more to do here myself."

"I'll think of you while I buy popcorn at the movies." He reached over and grabbed the latest edition of the paper, flipping through to find the theater ads. He suddenly forgot about going to the movies. "Patterson, your hair is a mess!"

"What?" She automatically ran both hands through it, trying to persuade it into order.

"Let's go have your hair done!"

"Look, Joe Malone, it's none of your business how my hair—"

"No insult intended. Read this," he said, thrusting the paper at her.

"'Singles-only night at Hair Amore.' That's an ultratrendy hair salon."

"No appointments necessary. Grab your notebook. You get an expense-account make-over, and I'll figure out how to make a date with a woman sitting under a hair dryer."

"There's nothing wrong with my look. I don't want to be made over. You're the one with shaggy hair."

"Come on, I'll drive. I got my muffler fixed." He tuned out her babble of protests and whisked her down to his car before he could have second thoughts.

4

It was a factory for transforming ordinary people into imitations of trendy high-fashion models. Chemical fumes permeated the air—solutions smelling like rotten fish, dyes reeking of ammonia.

"You were right!" Amy shouted over the pulsating beat of music distorted by hidden speakers. "A health club is a great place to meet people. Let's go find one."

"This has possibilities." She watched as Joe scanned the crowded room.

Hair Amore was staffed by an army of beauticians, male and female, all in black shorts and white tank tops. They were walking advertisements for their services—hair clipped, teased, lacquered, dyed and tortured into designs inspired by chic magazines. Mascara was the makeup of choice.

An emaciated receptionist in a black fishnet top took their names and thrust plastic wineglasses, the kind with screw-off bases, into their hands. Amy cautiously sniffed the pale liquid that half filled it. It resembled Chablis but could have been watered-down apple juice or perming solution. She took a tiny sip, but her taste buds seemed to be on strike.

She turned to say something else to Joe, but he was listening intently to a blonde with improbably long lashes and the chest measurement of a *Playboy* centerfold.

Nothing was lonelier than being the only person in a crowded room not talking to anyone. She spotted an empty chair in the reception area—black wrought iron with jungle-cat print cushions—and plopped down into it, pretending the wine was her first drink after forty-eight hours in the desert.

There seemed to be three or four women for every man. She looked around at the mirrored stations haphazardly arrayed in a huge room with highly polished hardwood floors. The female stylists outnumbered the male by about the same ratio.

Did any of these women really believe they were going to meet Mr. Right while their hair was slicked down with styling gel or piled high with rollers?

"Hello, are you Amy?"

She raised her eyes from a pair of thick, hairy legs, past a designer's black leather version of lederhosen, up to the broadly smiling face of a middle-aged man with his salt-and-pepper beard woven into tiny braids.

"I'm Fritz. I'll be your beauty consultant this evening." He reached out and rolled a strand of her hair between his thumb and finger. "A tad bit lifeless. I recommend lightening it just a shade, then a protein conditioner."

"No way—I mean, I don't color my hair. It's natural."

He frowned just long enough to register disapproval, then showed a full set of horsey teeth. "It's the cut that's really crucial. A gorgeous face like yours should be framed, not overwhelmed. This has to go." He grabbed a handful of hair on either side of her face.

"This stays!" She pushed his moist, beefy hands away from her face and frantically tried to spot Joe. He had two hair consultants fussing over him—both female. "Really, I like my hair this way."

"I'll just put you down for a shampoo and set. We want our clients to be happy," he said in a tone that ranked her taste on a level with glow-in-the-dark earrings. "Josie will be your stylist. She'll be with you as soon as she finishes a blow-dry."

"Forget it!" she said to his retreating back, but her words were lost in the din.

Joe had disappeared. Since this torturous experience definitely qualified as an expense-account item, she might as well have her hair washed while she waited for Joe to do his research.

A gum-chewing shampoo girl finally led her to a sink, and afterward she sat on a black vinyl chair with wet hair plastered over her ears until her official operator came to finish her off.

The men, she noticed, were led to a separate, more secluded area where only their hairdressers knew for sure if they tinted or permed their locks. Apparently, Joe was getting more specialized attention than she was. He emerged from the sink area swathed in a purple cape and sauntered into the male domain. One more thing infuriated her about her unwanted partner. He looked good no matter what he was wearing, including a plastic cape that would make Superman blush. Worse, he had a classic skull that didn't need a luxuriant growth of hair to make women size him up favorably. He even looked great with wet locks sticking to his head. Worst of all, he probably knew it. He hadn't been veiled under a towel like the usual drenched patron returning from the sinks.

"Hi, I'm Josie. I'll be your stylist this evening," a skinny young girl who looked about fifteen said.

Amy groaned inwardly and again leaped to the defense of her copper bob.

In spite of Joe's head start, Amy ended up waiting for him in the crowded reception area. Was his operator cutting each hair individually?

"There you are," she said with relief when he finally appeared, not looking noticeably different. She was beginning to feel invisible in the mostly female throng.

"Do you have enough material for the column?" he asked.

"I'll make do. I'm ready to leave." A statuesque redhead armed with two plastic goblets was bearing down on him. "Now."

"I'm ready, too," he said, taking her arm and steering her toward the exit. "Any more phone numbers and I won't remember who goes with which name."

"I don't want to pull you away from these enthusiastic admirers."

"No, that's all right," he said with mock weariness. "After all that action, I'm ready for your company."

"My soothing personality?"

"Your caustic wit. I'd hate to start believing I'm irresistible."

"It would be terrible if your ego swelled up like a hot-air balloon."

He didn't pick up the gauntlet, instead leading her to his fire-engine red sports car with the Minnesota license plate: NWSHND.

"I'm not sure whether we should talk about our impressions over dinner," he said, opening the door of his little convertible for her. "Maybe we'll have a sharper edge if we don't discuss what we're going to write."

"I don't remember dinner being part of this package."

"We both have to eat."

"Not together."

"You're in a bad mood because nobody tried to hit on you, aren't you?"

"You don't know that! You were too busy fending off love-starved females."

"You must have seen more of me than I saw of you."

"If you mean did I watch what you were up to—"

"It's okay to be grumpy," he said with mock sympathy, "when you're feeling neglected. But I did get a glimpse of you with some chubby guy in leather rompers."

"I didn't feel in the least neglected, and that was no one—just Fritz."

"Oh, the owner," he said dismissively. "You know, Amy, your problem is you act unapproachable. You scare men off by looking cool and aloof."

"I what?" Her yelp of outrage wasn't feigned.

"It's a compliment. I mean aloof, as in regal, high-class—"

"I didn't go to that hair mill to find a date. I don't know why I went!"

"We both went," he said with the irritating reasonableness of a teacher explaining something to a disruptive child, "to experience the frustration men and women face trying to connect."

"You didn't look frustrated," she groused.

"Is it my fault I'm naturally outgoing? Women respond to friendliness."

She clamped her mouth shut. Darned if she'd tell him they responded first to his lean, sexy body and movie-star rugged looks. His ego was already as pumped up as one of the advertising blimps that hover over sporting events.

"I have plenty of material for our first special on etiquette," he said as he pulled into traffic with unnerving nonchalance.

"Bully for you."

"Don't tell me you came up empty?"

"I like to digest situations before I rush to the computer."

"Let's have a sandwich at the Java Joint."

"Oh, might as well. I'll buy if—no, never mind."

"If I share my observations with you? That would be cheating, Patterson."

"How can we be partners if we don't collaborate?"

"Good point. Throw in a slice of peach pie, and I'll give you a few hints on what I'll be writing."

Once a low-key coffeehouse specializing in espresso, the Java Joint had gone mainstream with neon and chrome decor that was supposed to resemble an old-fashioned diner's. They'd missed the dinner crowd but not the onslaught of teenagers that took over on Friday nights.

Amy had been there once with Ed, the lecturing graduate student. He'd insisted they sit at one of the long communal tables so he could mingle with the little people, especially the underage female of the species. Amy couldn't help comparing him with Joe, who dazzled the frumpy hostess into giving them the last empty booth in a quiet back corner.

Their waiter wore thonged sandals and a long white apron wrapped around his middle. Amy ordered an avocado and cream cheese sandwich on Swedish rye.

"Lots of alfalfa sprouts," she requested, "and iced tea."

"I'll have ham and cheese on pumpernickel," Joe said, "and a near beer. Now," he said with the air of a man ready to get down to business, "here's the way I see—"

"Never mind. We don't need to talk about it."

"I thought you wanted to know my angle."

"I have an angle or two of my own to explore," she said smugly.

"If you're sure . . ."

"Positive."

"What kind of angle?" He leaned forward and put his arms, bare below the shoved-up sleeves of his shirt, on the edge of the black Formica table.

"Hmm, don't tell me you need to pick my mind to find a hook for your part of the piece."

"Actually, I may write about the pickup lines women use on men. Which ones are turnoffs and which really spark a man's interest."

"That's original," she said in a tone that told him the idea was adequate but not exciting. He knew darn well she hadn't heard any pickup lines from men that evening.

"Well, what's your idea? You act like you're guarding state secrets from an enemy spy."

"I guess you're not a spy, but you weren't eager to share with me when we left the hair place." She probably needed his input more than he needed hers, but this was war. "Hair Amore makes a fetish out of being up-to-the-minute, but the men and women there were playing the same old game—trying to find clever ways to connect with the opposite sex. Not even the techniques change much. Some of the lines I overheard were probably updated versions of come-ons used by singles at box socials a hundred years ago."

"So you don't think there's any such thing as nineties dating or nineties etiquette?"

"It's just a rehash of the same old thing," she said. "The scenery may change, but men's and women's needs don't."

"So you're dismissing women's new role in society, all the social changes of the late twentieth century? You don't think the dating game is any different because of them?"

"Not dismissing—only diminishing their importance in the mating ritual."

"I like it." He leaned back and smiled broadly.

"You agree with me?"

"Not at all. That's why it has good potential. You focus on the sameness. I stress the differences."

And I'll look stuffy and outdated, she thought to herself. Was she going to end up sounding like a repressed spinster?

"I'll think about it some more," she said glumly.

"I can use the come-on lines I gathered tonight to show that women's needs have changed. They're looking for a new kind of relationship."

"You're beginning to sound like a diehard feminist," she said, wondering why she was always the one who was unseated in her jousts with Joe. She'd thrown out an idea from the top of her head, and he was running with it for a touchdown.

Their food came, and Amy welcomed the diversion. She made an elaborate ritual out of cutting the crusts off her bulky sandwich and replacing the sprouts that fell out.

He was watching her instead of eating.

"Are you going to eat your crusts?"

"I'll see how full I get."

"You eat the best part first, and only eat the crusts if you're still hungry?"

"Something like that." His scrutiny was making her too self-conscious to eat at all.

"My mother always said the crusts would put hair on my chest."

"Mothers must belong to some secret society where they learn all those myths. My mother's favorite was, 'Oatmeal will clear up your complexion.'"

"She must know something. You have beautiful skin."

"Oh, I wasn't—I mean—"

"You mean you weren't fishing. I know that, but I didn't know compliments would make you tongue-tied. Valuable piece of info. Well worth buying your dinner."

"Thank you—I think." She took a tiny bite of her sandwich, hoping none of the little green alfalfa leaflets would stick to her teeth. Now where had that worry come from?

"I'm glad you didn't let the hair people talk you into one of those weird styles. You've got it right already," he said.

Two compliments in a row! If he was trying to confuse her, he was succeeding!

"Thank you. Is your sandwich all right?"

He hadn't touched it, and she wasn't going to be able to swallow her first bite with those azure blue eyes watching her so intently. Funny, she'd never noticed the way his pupils captured the light, almost as though they were focused on tiny distant stars. She had a warm, funny feeling that shouldn't be happening with Joe Malone.

The moment passed. He started eating, talking about the Cubs' spring training between bites. She didn't have any consequential insights into baseball, but she was fascinated by his haircut. Dark mahogany locks softened his broad forehead just as they had before their session at Hair Amore. She was almost willing to swear the soft finger curls brushed his back collar exactly as they had before their visit to the salon.

"Do I have a mustard mustache?" he asked, catching her as she studied his hair.

"No! I mean no, I just can't see any difference in your hair after all that time in the men-only room."

"I explained that I was there to do research, not get clipped. The girls were nice about not cutting it. I had it washed and dried so their feelings wouldn't be hurt."

"Very kind, I'm sure," she said wryly. She just bet the "girls" were nice!

The waitress cleared away her pile of crusts and Joe's empty plate, then brought them demitasses. The caffeine jolt didn't work its magic; for a night person Amy was fading fast. Across from her, Joe still looked depressingly unwilted for someone who claimed to be a morning person. His slight five o'clock shadow only enhanced the appeal of his strong chin and full lips.

She tried to stifle a yawn but wasn't successful.

"I'm tired, too," Joe said. "It's been a long day. Of course, if we were on a date, I might think you were bored."

"I'll try to remember not to yawn too much when we go on our pretend 'real date.'"

"We need to start planning it first thing Monday morning."

He actually seemed to perk up when he reminded her of their assignment. He was going to enjoy watching her squirm through it! Why did she keep getting flashbacks to her high school days when she was a geeky sophomore? Her love/hate nonrelationship with the worldly senior who'd beaten her out of the editor's job had colored her life for one turbulent year, but it was ancient history, forgotten long ago and of no consequence now. So why did he make her feel the same way she had felt then?

"Let's go," she said.

He paid the bill, then drove to the nearly deserted *Monitor* parking lot, stopping a short distance from her car.

"Thanks for the ride," she said automatically, opening the passenger-side door before he came to a complete stop.

"Don't be so eager to get away. I'll walk you to your car."

"It's right there."

"Are you running away from me?" he asked, catching up as she reached her car door.

"Of course not. I'm going home."

She had her key in hand, but for a crazy moment she looked into his face and forgot what to do with it. The photo session seemed a million light-years away, but she had an eerie sensation that the imprint of Joe's lips was still on hers, as though he'd just finished kissing her.

The sodium vapor security lights cast a brownish glow on everything that had red hues, so hopefully her face only looked dirty, not scarlet from blushing.

He'd pushed his hands into his pockets again, pulling his trousers tight against his hipbones, and she suddenly thought this boyish habit was arousing.

Fatigue was making her giddy! Why did Joe Malone have to come back into her life just as gorgeous—and exasperating—as he had been twelve years ago?

"Thank you," she said again, trying to end the evening on a conventionally polite note.

"For what?" His expression was too shadowy for her to read.

"For not making me stay at singles' night forever," she answered lamely, wondering if she should thank him for a dinner he was going to put on his expense account. Or was he? When did work stop and real life begin? How was she going to sort this out when she was with Joe?

"No problem," he said casually. "I think we both learned something tonight."

She was afraid to ask what. The keyhole evaded her hesitant thrust, and she had to locate it with her thumb before she could unlock her car door. Everything she did around Malone made her look like a klutz!

He opened the door for her, but her motor skills were frozen. She couldn't seem to execute the maneuver necessary to get behind the steering wheel.

"Good night," he said in a soft, husky voice that would have given her goose bumps from someone she really wanted to be with.

"'Night," she said to his retreating back.

If they'd been on a date, she thought, he would have lost points for making her think he was going to kiss her—then not doing it.

She couldn't wait to see how his scoreboard would look when they started "dating."

"Let's go home," she muttered to her steering wheel. Too much had happened too fast. Her circuits were overloaded, but she didn't want to give Joe credit for the electrical tingles coursing through her.

Joe never went near the office on Saturday for anything less than a major emergency. He didn't know why a crazy impulse had brought him there at noon today. He did find what he expected—Amy holed up in their cubicle, intent on the computer screen in front of her.

His rubber-soled running shoes didn't make a sound on the hard tiles, and he stood watching her from the doorway without attracting her attention. Her vibrant coppery hair was pulled up into a short ponytail, exposing her nape. He shifted his peace offering from one hand to the other and repressed a strong urge to sneak up and kiss her there. How would it feel to let his hands linger on her smooth, tanned shoulders left bare by a pale pink tank top?

She probably would kill me, he thought with a grin, almost convincing himself it was worth the risk to taste that warm, silky skin.

Instead, he called up images of bearding a lioness in her den, picturing her as a snarling feline straight from a public television nature documentary.

He cleared his throat noisily so she wouldn't accuse him of sneaking up on her. "Hard at it, I see."

"What are you doing in the office on Saturday morning?" she asked, half-turning in her chair to look at him.

"Make that afternoon," he corrected her. "It's ten past noon."

"I thought you might be busy following up on all the phone numbers you collected at Hair Amore."

She couldn't say good-morning without hurling a challenge at him! Instead of tickling the back of her neck with the bouquet of flowers he'd impulsively bought for her, he tossed them on the desk beside her computer.

"Late sleepers usually make the best dates, so I never call in the morning," he said, in hopes of making her yelp. She didn't deserve to know he'd tossed all the numbers when he cleaned out his pockets last night. Maybe he should retrieve them from the trash. He was in the mood for some fun-filled, uncomplicated dating.

"Flowers? For the office?" She actually looked confused.

"I'm not in the habit of buying them for myself."

"Are they for me?"

When he nodded, she picked them up and pulled the green tissue away from the stems.

Watching her bury her nose in the yellow daisies, white carnations and baby's breath was more than worth the few bucks he'd paid for them. Damn! He would be better off working with the original Holly Heartfelt. He'd never met her, but he imagined gray hair, thick glasses and orthopedic shoes. At least with her as a partner, he'd be able to keep his mind on business.

"I just picked them up on the way over," he said more gruffly than he intended.

"Thank you, Joe. They're beautiful." She plucked a daisy and tucked it behind her ear, anchoring it in her pulled-back hair. He wished she hadn't done that. It made her look so... He ran through his extensive vocabulary and could only come up with "desirable." And that was the last thing he wanted in a partner—to be constantly reminded that she was one hundred percent feminine under her work-obsessed exterior.

"A peace offering," he said, "for dragging you to Hair Amore. It was nothing but a cattle market—okay for guys on the make but demeaning to women."

He looked around the office, hoping to see something that would serve as a vase. It was getting to him, watching Amy sniff and caress the flowers.

"How did you know I would be in the office?" she asked, sticking the bouquet into her half-empty bottle of spring water.

"A hunch."

"Hey, what's this?" She pulled out a yellow envelope of powdered drink mix that was staked in with the greenery in the bouquet.

"Lemonade," Joe said, reading the package.

"Yes, but what's it doing in the flowers?"

"I bought them at a grocery store," he admitted. "It's probably some kind of promotion—lemonade with yellow flowers, cherry drink with red."

"Or were you trying to tell me I'm as sour as a lemon?"

"Choose your own interpretation." He grinned. "But I really didn't notice the packet when I bought them."

"Then thank you again. Did you come here just to deliver flowers?"

"Would you believe me if I said yes?"

She arched one eyebrow but didn't answer.

He didn't feel like working, but he sat at his terminal just so she wouldn't attach too much significance to the flowers. After all, buying them had been only a crazy impulse. He should have remembered that women tended to make a big deal out of any gift they classified as romantic. Somehow, though, he had trouble fitting Patterson into the typical-woman category.

He reluctantly put some of his ideas into the computer, but this wasn't how he wanted to spend Saturday afternoon.

"Let me see yours, and I'll show you mine," he suggested when he had a few paragraphs roughed out.

"I don't know..."

"You are working on something for the column, aren't you? If you're keeping a secret diary or writing a clandestine novel—"

"Don't be silly. Read it, if you insist."

They traded places, and he could tell she'd been hard at work for hours. Her stuff was so good he made a game of trying to find something wrong with it.

Gotcha! he thought, then loudly called out, "A split infinitive!"

"No!" She dashed from her seat and leaned over his shoulder, filling his nostrils with the fresh, flowery scent of her hair and skin. "Darn! You're right!" A few minutes later, she had her turn. "Aha! A run-on sentence!"

"I never do that," he grumbled, getting up and leaning over her shoulder.

He had the devil's own time concentrating on his scintillating prose when he was so close to her nape. He moved even nearer, letting his chin graze the top of her head, enjoying the tickling sensation of her hair on his skin. He rested his hands on either side of her on the worn leather armrests of the chair and tried to pretend he cared what he was reading.

She edged forward, and the chair buckled, nearly spilling her on the floor. He reached out and caught her, holding her firm, luscious arms against her sides.

"Maybe we should read just for content," she suggested. "This is only rough copy."

"Rough," he agreed, thinking how hard it was to withdraw his hands.

He needed either a roll in the hay with a lusty lass or a Minnesota shower—cold, cold, cold. If he started thinking of Patterson as a woman, every workday was going to be a hundred hours long.

He backed off, trying to read with professional detachment, but her style made him smile. Her quirky sensitivity came though in her writing, but he didn't want to say anything about it until she reacted to his work.

"I hate to admit it," she said at last, "but I shouldn't have worried about your sense of humor. I was afraid you'd try for laughs when people really needed help. But your humorous touch works, Malone. This is good stuff."

He was inordinately pleased by her praise but irritated with himself because her opinion mattered so much to him.

"I appreciate that," he said slowly, "because you really know what you're doing."

Did he only imagine that the back of her neck got pinker?

"I'm going to quit now," he said. "Want to go to lunch?"

"No, thanks. I'm going to stay until I've finished sorting these letters. I like to start Monday without any backlog."

She didn't ask him to help; he didn't volunteer.

"See you Monday," he said, leaving without a backward glance.

He was glad he wasn't seriously interested in dating her. Her workaholic ways would drive him crazy.

5

Amy headed into the Monday-morning rush hoping traffic wouldn't be stalled. There was no reason why she had to get to the office before Joe; it just made her feel better to be hard at work when he strolled in.

"What are you trying to prove?" she asked herself, lowering the window to enjoy the cool air while it lasted. The best thing about the desert climate was the sharp drop in temperature when the sun went down, making every morning a perfect new beginning.

She turned and immediately got stuck behind a lumbering old dump truck hauling a load of rubble. Her lane was advancing at a crawl, and the chance of getting into the next one was a fender-bending one in eighty.

She had a superstition. A bad Monday morning was an omen. If things went wrong then, the whole week would be the pits. Silly, of course, she thought as she craned her neck hoping for an opening in the faster-moving line of vehicles beside her.

This was her idea of purgatory—being stuck in a car endlessly inching forward in snarled traffic, unable to see around a dilapidated truck in front of her. All she could do was enjoy the scenery—on a street with nothing but commercial buildings, poky little eating places and dives with neon beer signs in dark windows. Then, miracle of miracles, the truck turned right and gave her an unobstructed view of...

"Oh, no!"

The billboard towering up from the flat roof of a wholesale food distributor's warehouse dominated the skyline. Only last Friday the same sign had teased thirsty motorists with a ten-foot-high mug of foamy beer. Now it was slowing traffic as drivers gawked at a pair of female legs—*her* legs—blown up to gigantic proportions. Why on earth had she worn that tight little dress? It made her rear look like something that belonged on a calendar in a men's locker room. Worst of all, a giant Joe was attacking her lips with so much gusto she could almost hear the kiss.

She was past the billboard before she recovered enough to realize she hadn't even read the message.

How could this happen to her? She must be imagining things! No one could put up a billboard that fast!

One man could: William Ranson III, owner and publisher of the *Monitor*, lord over half of Phoenix. If he said, "Dance," half a million pairs of feet would start twitching.

"I only got a glimpse. It couldn't be as bad as I think," she said, raising her window in a turtlelike gesture, pretending it was a shell that would hide her from the world. As if anyone would notice whether the babe on the billboard had a face!

How did they make billboards? Surely some artist who specialized in girlie magazines had done a job on her. At least they'd put it up on the dingy fringe of the city where no one would take much notice of it.

She passed two more of the same traffic-slowing billboards before she reached the *Monitor* parking lot. Joe was the sexiest giant since Calvin Klein started making underwear. Even his feet looked macho in those scruffy old boots.

Two people tooted at her as she scurried through the lot toward the entrance. She responded to their waves with a halfhearted flick of her wrist.

She was going to burn that dress!

As if she needed one more ominous Monday omen, she found Joe in the office ahead of her.

"Don't say anything," she warned, rushing to the file and pulling out the faded pink sweater. Why had she picked today to wear a clingy white silk top with a short black skirt? She would have given a day's pay to go home and change into her interview suit.

"You looked—" Joe began.

"Don't say it!"

"Incredibly sexy." He picked up their phone and answered a quick series of questions. "I'll have to confirm it with my partner, but tomorrow looks good. Get back to you." He turned to Amy. "Dana DeJong's morning show," he said. "I'll call her back as soon as we clear our schedule with Bug."

"We're supposed to go on her television show?"

"Yes, but I'm more excited about our segment on the evening news, although her show does get good ratings."

"Evening news?" Her voice squeaked.

"The phone's been ringing off the hook."

It rang again as if on cue, and Joe tentatively committed them to an interview on an FM radio station.

"Joe, stop that right now!"

"What?" He frowned at her sweater. "Are you cold again?"

"No—yes! Stop making appointments for us without consulting me!"

"Amy, we'll have to go over the whole schedule with Garver. All these dates are tentative." He waved a notepad at her.

The phone shrilled yet again, and he reached for it.

"Don't answer that!"

"You take it then."

That was an even worse idea. "No, go ahead."

"For you." He handed her the receiver.

"Hello... oh, you did. You do?"

She didn't talk long.

"You'll have to get used to fans. You're not the anonymous voice of Holly Heartfelt anymore," Joe said.

"That was no fan—that was my mother. She liked it."

"Why wouldn't she? Her little girl is famous."

"I don't want to be famous. All I want is to pay my rent without getting some psycho for a roommate. This—this *fiasco* has to stop!"

"Read your contract, Patterson. Promotion is part of the big picture."

She cringed when he said "big picture."

It was early afternoon before they had time to sit down together and work on trivial details like the contents of their hotshot new column, renamed Two Views.

"We'd better plan our first date," Joe said.

Did he know his electric blue broadcloth shirt made his eyes look like deep azure pools? Of course he did! He was loving his role as a billboard sensation, and he'd probably planned his outfit to match a celebrity image. His black jeans fit like a second skin. She could see right through him. He made casual dressing into an art form.

"Where should we go?" She meant, *Where can we go without being recognized as the billboard bodies?*

"Let's start with dinner at a nice restaurant," he suggested.

"We can go into the mountains. Flagstaff—Flagstaff would be nice. Blackie's Saloon has great atmosphere." Fugitives always went into the hills to hide; it was an Arizona tradition.

"We could," he said dubiously, "but why drive more than two hours there and two back on a first date? We have to pretend we know nothing about each other."

"Pretend," she said frantically, fervently wishing she really didn't know him.

She didn't need him complicating her life. How should she handle being a king-size pinup? She'd planned to sign up for water aerobics with some women friends, and she could imagine their curiosity about the sexy hunk on the billboard. They'd make the pool water boil!

"Why do I get the impression you're not really with me?" he asked.

"Oh, I'm definitely with you." They'd go down in history together, his lips locked on hers as she twitched with shock—or anticipation. "This has to be a weeknight date. It's a standard first-date ploy. Then if things aren't going well, either one of us can use work as an excuse to leave early—either half of the couple we're pretending to be, I mean."

"Are you planning to end our evening early so you can beat me to work the next morning?"

"I got tied up in traffic this morning."

"You probably tied up traffic—at least, the ten-foot version of you did."

"I don't want to talk about the billboard." She was sure he knew that. "A lunch date is another option."

"Let's go with dinner. This week is going to be hectic. How about Thursday? The uproar will die down by then. We'll have had our fifteen minutes of fame."

"Fine. Where do you want to go?"

"I'll let you choose the restaurant. I'll eat anything— except your leftover crusts."

"Funny, Joe, really funny. I'll think about it and tell you later."

He was "letting" her do another job he didn't want to do.

* * *

Joe didn't beat Amy to work again that week. He didn't try. Fortunately, his laptop computer was compatible with the model at the paper, so he roughed out his copy at home before he went in to the office to handle the activity created by the Big Board, as everyone on the *Monitor* now called it. He liked writing without distractions—especially without the proximity of his partner. Her slender, ivory-colored arm was too close to his shoulder when he sat at his terminal. He was constantly tempted to tip his chair just enough to brush against it—except when she wore that awful pink thing. He was thinking of hiding it—or buying her something large and tentlike to cut down on the temptation level. Even her ugly sweater carried the subtle scent of a perfume that teased his nostrils whenever he was in the tiny cubicle.

She grumbled when he didn't come in until after ten Thursday morning, but she couldn't complain about his output. He was carrying his share of the load. In fact, keeping up with his workaholic partner put them ahead of schedule on daily columns, and the etiquette series was ready to debut Sunday with a piece on the trials and tribulations of meeting people. Their different reactions to singles' night at the hair salon made good reading, in his opinion. It was sure to be controversial enough to bring in lots of letters.

They hadn't talked about their big first date since she'd mentioned her restaurant choice on Tuesday. If she'd shown any enthusiasm, he might be looking forward with pleasure to an evening with his feisty copper-haired partner. As it was, she made the dinner seem like an extension of their already-hectic workday.

He had to give her credit for the way she was handling the publicity generated by the billboards. She was rocky before their first public appearance, but once she got her sense of humor back, they both breezed through a whole series of dumb-question interviews.

"I'll pick you up at your apartment around seven, if that's okay," he said, wondering why it was so hard to sound casual about it.

"Don't bother. I'll just meet you at the restaurant."

"Why not go right from here? You can squeeze in an extra hour of drudgery."

"On a real date, I'd go home and change. Or maybe bring some going-out things to the office and dress here. But I didn't think of that, so I guess I'll have to go home."

"Don't go to too much trouble," he said dryly.

"Fine, I'll meet you—"

"No. If we meet at the restaurant, how can I pass those all-important first-date tests like arriving promptly and opening the car door?"

"Okay, pick me up."

"Seven?"

"Fine."

He'd been dating ever since he stopped spending all his available cash on baseball cards, but it had never seemed so complicated, not even when he was still young enough to worry whether it was cool to kiss a girl with his mouth open.

Where did the touchy-feely stuff come in on these mock dates with Patterson? It wouldn't be a realistic situation if he didn't at least think of sampling those creamy peach lips, or maybe holding her in his arms so he could feel her luscious breasts pressed against his chest. He didn't want her barbed prose to describe him as a woman-hater or a eunuch, but he wasn't sure what would happen if he let himself take her in his arms. How far was she willing to go to gather material for their series?

"I guess that's settled, then. Is there anything else we should talk about?" he asked, hoping for some helpful hints from her.

"Like you said, all settled," she said in a monotone.

He peeked at her screen. Did she know she was rereading copy they'd turned in two days ago?

Amy did little besides check the time from four o'clock on. How could he do this to her? Normally he was the first one to leave the building. Today the second hand crept around the dial on her wristwatch with excruciating slowness, but when five o'clock finally came, he still hadn't budged. All he was doing was reading a stack of women's magazines he'd borrowed for research. Why choose this day to plant his rear on the desk chair and stay overtime?

She didn't want Joe to see what time it was when she left work. Any other day, her plan to leave early would have worked. She wanted extra prep time to get ready for their date, but she didn't want him to know about it. Even a pretend date with a co-worker was awkward!

Was he deliberately lingering to see when she left? Would she flunk some first-date test if she rushed home to change at the last possible moment?

"Are you reading something interesting?" she asked, breaking a long silence between them.

"No, mostly I'm admiring the ads. Never knew there was so much skin in women's magazines."

His grin gave him away. He was playing games with her.

"I think I'll stop for groceries on the way home," she lied.

"No need. We're in such good graces right now, we can order lobster at the *Monitor*'s expense."

He knew she wanted time to look good, but he showed no sign of leaving.

She retrieved her purse from the file and thought of another place she could pretend to go.

"Forgot the cleaners closes at six. I'd better go."

"If you need more time to get ready..."

"Oh, no. See you at seven."

Even without making stops, she really had to rush. Why didn't she agree to a later time? Recently she'd read a magazine poll claiming women spent more time getting ready for first dates than any others. Even though she knew it was a work assignment, she wanted to go through the whole ritual from head to foot. After all, a critique on her appearance could appear in the column if Joe wanted to be a stinker.

She brought a bad case of pre-date jitters home with her, and she still had to make the big decision—what to wear. She waffled between outfits, considering everything in the closet except her black suit and the billboard dress. With the clock hands moving at double time, she finally decided on a wheat-colored sheath dress with a matching long jacket. The hemline ended above midthigh, but otherwise it was conservative enough for a job interview. She wasn't sure what message she wanted to project, but the high neckline and long sleeves were ladylike in the extreme. Would Joe think she was too timid or too stuffy?

She'd just decided to change when the doorbell sounded.

Joe was there.

She didn't want to go.

Yes, she did! She just didn't want it to be an assignment.

She rushed to the door, took a deep breath, and counted to ten before opening it.

"Hi." Should she invite him into her apartment or go right out?

"Hello." He drawled the word, giving himself time for the "look."

He thought she looked bland; she could read it in his expression. Only her legs got an appreciative second glance. Great! The only part of her that impressed her "date" would be hidden under the table all night.

* * *

Joe knew the moment called for some kind of comment, something to put his companion at ease and set the tone for a first date. But conventional chitchat never felt right with Amy; he always felt pressured to be clever and original. Was it because they were both writers? Were they both so competitive that every word between them had to score points? Or was she just special?

"You look really nice," he said, knowing how mundane that sounded.

"Thank you."

"That's your date talking. Your office mate thinks you picked the perfect outfit—an ice-princess dress, demure but still seductive because it leaves so much to the imagination. Short enough to be eye-catching."

"Thank you, I think."

"I'll say anything to see you blush."

"Whenever you say something nice, you have to add a smart remark so I won't take you seriously," she complained.

"Do I do that? Sorry, it's not intentional. Can I start over? Hello, I'm Joe Malone. You look lovely tonight."

"So do you. I like your suit."

"Thanks." He didn't tell her he'd bought it especially for their date. Of course, it didn't hurt to have a charcoal gray for job interviews in case the column bombed, but he really didn't think it would.

He did everything by the book on the trip from her apartment to the restaurant: holding doors, making small talk, laughing at the right times. What he didn't do was analyze the flush of pride he felt walking into the Silver Swan with Amy on his arm.

She'd made a good restaurant choice; it was upscale but not ostentatious. The owners had tried for an English-pub ambience, not surprising in the state that had hauled London Bridge across the ocean.

"Table for two for Malone," he said to a dignified maître d' with silver hair slicked back without a part.

"I'm sorry, sir. We don't have a reservation in that name."

"Did you use your name?" Joe asked Amy.

"Me? I thought you called for reservations."

"You picked the place. I assumed you made them. How long a wait?" he asked the maître d'.

"At least three hours, sir, and I can't guarantee it won't be longer."

"On a Thursday?" Joe pulled out a five-dollar bill, surprised when the man shook his head.

"We have two private parties this evening. There are no tables available."

"We can go somewhere else," Amy said.

"Either that or call this a breakfast date." He pulled a ten-dollar bill from his money clip.

"We can write about what a fiasco first dates can be," she suggested.

"Garver would not be pleased." In truth, Malone wouldn't be pleased, either. He didn't want the evening to end before it started. "Are you sure you can't squeeze us in somewhere?"

"Let's go, Joe," she urged. "I'll take the blame for not making reservations."

"No, my fault. I should have asked."

"Let's worry about it later. You can choose some other place."

Apparently the firebrand of the newsroom was timid when it came to restaurant politics, but he wasn't going to up the bribe again when the ten was refused.

It was only a short drive to Tommy O'Malley's, and they were ushered immediately to one of the booths with high-backed seats upholstered in dusty rose velvet. The servers were dressed in costumes, all representing the real or fictitious Wild West: Calamity Jane, Miss Kitty from

"Gunsmoke," Wyatt Earp, Buffalo Bill and other legendary figures.

"Well, what do you think?" he asked.

"Not exactly what I'd choose for a first date. It's maybe a little hokey."

"You suggested Blackie's Saloon. They have a Western theme."

"I only wanted to go there because there are no Big Boards in Flagstaff," she emphasized.

"This place is right off the freeway, not too far from your apartment in case you want to bail out by using the 'early to work' excuse."

Before Amy could say anything else, a saloon girl in red satin came to take their orders.

"I know you!" she said excitedly. "You're the guy on those billboards! Oh, do you mind? I want my friend to see you. Brenda, look who's here!"

Her counterpart in lavender satin hurried over, breasts heaving and bustle flouncing. "I just love your billboards. Would you mind terribly signing a menu for me?"

Joe signed two menus, mentioning that Amy was on the billboards, too. She added her signature below his, her expression reminding him of icicles hanging on a front porch in Minneapolis.

"Nice girls," Joe said mildly when their waitress went off, to fetch Amy's white wine and his mineral water, he hoped. He was thirsty, but he wanted to be totally clear-headed this evening.

"The lavender belle nearly toppled over on your lap when you asked her name." She took out a pad and made a pencil notation.

"Don't tell me you're taking notes."

"I don't want to forget—"

"You're forgetting to have a good time. That's why we're here."

"We're here for research. How can I remember whether you've passed all those important first-date tests if I don't take notes?"

He wasn't buying the innocent way she fluttered her eyelashes. "I'll take a written test later. Aren't you worried about flunking some of my criteria?"

She dropped the pencil and pad back into her purse. "What am I doing wrong?"

"You're not focused on me," he said.

"How can I be when you encourage waitresses to—"

"From now on you have my total attention. I've never been a celebrity before. For a minute there, I enjoyed it, but no more. We need to practice the art of first-date conversation. You first."

"Why me?"

"All right, I'll start. Do you think the Cubs should—"

"No, Joe! Not sports."

"You like basketball, so I thought—"

"That's beside the point. We're on a first date. Talking sports is a man thing. You can't assume a woman follows baseball. You have to use a more personal approach."

"Okay, consider my wrist slapped on that one. May I assume you read newspapers?"

"You lose points for sarcasm."

"The old standard, then. What do you like to do when you're not working?" He snorted, doubting whether she had time for anything but her job.

"Lots of things. I read a lot. I may take a water aerobics class. I play a little tennis."

"You just told me not to mention sports."

"It's okay after you learn whether your date is interested."

"Is there some rule book I don't know about?"

"Of course not. Just be your usual charming, fascinating self."

"If I start talking about my charming, fascinating self, you'll dock me points for being an egomaniac."

She giggled, then their drinks arrived, giving him an instant to think.

He took several time-consuming sips, then tried again. "I have a tattoo."

"Why did you get it?"

"Wrong, Amy, wrong! You're supposed to ask where it is or what it is."

"Who, what, where, when, how and why. We journalists get to them all eventually."

"'Why' is a challenge. It sounds like you're asking, Why do a dumb thing like that? 'What' shows you're interested. 'Where' shows you're *really* interested."

"Let me guess. You got drunk in college and had a dragon tattooed on your rear."

"You got the college part right. My budget at the time didn't allow for dragons. I settled for a phoenix. I always liked the legend of the mythical bird rising out of the ashes."

"And you grew up in Phoenix. Not as bad as a snake tattoo, I guess."

The lady-in-red came to take their dinner orders. Amy chose veal Parmesan; he went with blackened swordfish.

"I think you're spoofing about the tattoo," she said as soon as the waitress had left.

"What makes you think so?"

"It's the kind of trick you'd pull."

"This is our first date, remember? You're not supposed to know anything about me."

"You can know someone as a friend, then go on a first date."

"No, our premise is that we're strangers."

"Well, do you have one?"

He laughed.

"You don't!"

He smiled.

"Joe Malone, tell me the truth. Do you have a tattoo?"

"Got you thinking about body parts, didn't I?"

"You made it up! You don't have one!"

"I didn't say that. We're strangers who just met. This conversation is probably too intimate. Next you'll be telling me you have a birthmark shaped like a duck on your tush."

"You're incorrigible! I'm going to write about nightmare first dates."

"Aren't you afraid of hurting my feelings?"

"Oh..."

"Saved by the salads." He remembered why he didn't like to bring dates here. The service was too fast. He was enjoying Amy's company, even if she did give him a zero rating as a first date.

He watched as she dribbled a small amount of French dressing over her salad. She passed the selection of dressings to him, but he was more interested in watching her than in eating.

"Well, what's the answer? The question was, aren't you afraid of hurting my feelings?"

Her fork speared a piece of lettuce and a cherry tomato.

"No."

"Just no? You never answer a question with one word. You explain, expand, beat the subject to death."

"That's not true." She brought the fork to her mouth, opening her lips to take a bite. The little tomato squirted, and a sliver of lettuce fell away from the utensil. "Oh, no!"

The oily lettuce landed dead center on the front of her dress. She gingerly picked it off, leaving an orange stain on the light, silky fabric.

"There's something for you to write about—sloppy dates," she said with a groan.

"I won't do that," he promised. "Don't try to wipe it off. It will only spread. Leave it for the dry cleaners."

"You sound like an expert."

"I am. All I have to do is put on a tie, and food rains down from above."

"You're just being nice. I should go sponge this."

"Won't help. Might make it worse."

She shrugged and took another bite of salad.

"Congratulations," he said.

"For being sloppy?"

"For sloughing off a minor mishap. I hate it when women act as if smeared lipstick or a loose button is a major crisis."

"Especially when you're responsible? No, cross that out. Don't watch me eat."

"What?"

"You're watching me chew. Am I doing it wrong?"

"Eating is eating. I didn't know there was a rule in the books for that, too."

"To get back to our conversation," she said, "family is always a safe subject."

He spooned blue cheese dressing over his salad. "Okay, tell me about yours."

"You already know all there is to know. You and Sonny were friends for years."

"And if we weren't friends, would I care what he's doing? Family isn't a hot topic, Patterson."

"I'm open to suggestions," she said coolly.

"Work. I like talking about work."

"We do the same thing."

"If you didn't have a taboo against dating fellow workers, we might have plenty to talk about—people, policies, anecdotes."

"All right, I'll try. Have you met Bug's secretary? I heard she got in an argument last week with an ad rep."

He smiled broadly, not caring what they talked about. Listening to her was almost as much fun as watching her.

Dinner came all too quickly, and it was over before he wanted it to be. He even ordered dessert—chocolate cheesecake—to make the meal last longer, but he couldn't talk her into an ice-cream drink. When the waitress brought the check, he reached for it.

"Just a minute. Aren't we going to write about the economics of dating? Should we assume the man always pays?"

"If this were a real date, I'd expect to buy dinner."

"But do all men still expect to pay? Think nineties, Joe."

"Right. You're the conservative—I'm the voice of today. You can pay and wait for the *Monitor* to reimburse you."

She didn't look especially happy about winning, but she picked up the leather folder holding their tab.

"New wrinkle." She frowned. "The waitress left you a tip." She waved a slip of paper. "Phone number from the lavender belle."

"Thanks." He crumpled it and tried to stick it in his pocket but couldn't. He'd forgotten that better jackets always came with the pockets sewn shut.

Amy noticed, of course.

"New suit?"

"Yeah." He put the note in his trouser pocket.

"Nice, but you just lost points big-time."

"Because my pockets are stitched shut?"

"No, that's flattering, wearing a new suit for our date. But you should have tossed the phone number in the ashtray."

"We're in the nonsmoking section. We don't have one. Anyway, why hurt the girl's feelings?"

"We have to review word usage here—girls, ladies, women. When do you use which?"

Sometimes he wanted to shake her; most of the time he just wanted to get his hands on her any way he could.

Amy felt lighthearted, even giddy. She'd dropped oily lettuce on her dress, watched waitresses pant over Joe and verbally fenced with him throughout the whole meal. She should write the date off as a disaster, but she'd had an incredibly good time.

"I guess this is where we agree that tomorrow is a workday," he said when they got to his car.

"Guess so."

The drive to her apartment took only minutes, not nearly enough time for her to decide whether to ask him up for coffee.

He found a parking spot near her brightly lit entrance and killed the motor. "I'll walk you to your door, of course."

"You don't need to."

He ignored her halfhearted protest and came around to the passenger side of the car. She waited until he opened the door for her.

Before she could take a step toward the entrance, he caught her hand in his, holding it as they walked. Was this a friendly hand-hold or a preliminary gesture that would lead to something? He parted her fingers and slipped his between them, then caressed the top of her hand with his fingertips. Somehow his thumb found the thin-skinned area of her wrist. Was he taking her pulse? Her heart was pumping like a sprinter's. Would he think she was excited because he was touching her?

Her mind said pull away, but her hand was too busy basking in his warm, sensuous grip to do the sensible thing.

"Do you have your key?"

She didn't even remember climbing the stairs to her floor.

"Oh, sure." She fumbled but couldn't seem to open the catch with her left hand while the bag was hanging from her left shoulder.

Reluctantly she removed her right hand from his and dug to the bottom of her purse to find her key ring.

"Let me."

She recognized the expression on his face; every man put one on like that. It meant he wanted to kiss her. She closed her eyes for an instant, but nothing happened. He'd turned toward the door and was opening it.

"You don't have to ask me in for coffee," he said.

The invitation had been on the tip of her tongue.

"I guess I shouldn't, not with a stranger on a first date."

"I'll worry about your survival instincts if you do. After all, what do you really know about me—your date, that is."

"Well, I didn't run a credit check or investigate your background for possible felony convictions."

"Exactly. A girl—woman—has to be careful these days."

"Is that what you're going to put in the piece?"

"I thought you could handle the safety advice."

"Yes, I'm supposed to be the conservative voice." Why did she feel so let down?

He had that mushy look again. It was sappy on guys she didn't want to kiss, but on Joe it seemed special. She batted her eyelashes—where had that gesture come from? She pursed her lips. She stood straighter, knowing her new bra made her breasts stand at attention. She even lifted her heels off the floor to make herself taller, easier to reach. She'd never been so ready to be kissed—or so disappointed when he abruptly said good-night and bounded away from her.

"I'll call," he yelled back.

"Oh, big deal," she muttered as she closed the door behind her. "You men always say that."

Joe had nearly kissed her; she would swear to it. So she'd had a narrow escape. She knew how his kisses felt. The whole city was witness to the oomph he could put into them. If he had kissed her—if she had let him kiss her—their lives would be messy and complicated. He'd be there in the office tomorrow. They would pretend nothing had happened, but they'd watch each other continually, asking the big question: What next? It might even lead to the Big Thing. Then their working relationship would be hopelessly compromised.

Office romances were bad news. How many times did she have to get stung to learn her lesson?

She stomped into her clothing-strewn bedroom, remembering how she'd agonized over what to wear. She couldn't peel off the stained dress quickly enough.

All this emotional turmoil boiled down to one thing. She was mad. Not at Joe; not even at herself. She was just mad.

6

Amy was nearly ready to leave for the office the next morning when the phone rang.

"Hello." She could feel her heart beating in anticipation, even though there was no reason to suspect it was Joe. Weird sensation!

"Hi, Amy. What's up?"

She hated it when a man started a phone conversation without giving his name first, as though she got calls from only one male in the whole universe. Unfortunately, this voice didn't make her heart skip a beat.

"I'm on my way to work. Who is this?"

"Ed."

She'd guessed right.

"I wondered what you're doing tomorrow night," he said.

"Tomorrow—Saturday. Oh, sorry, Ed. I'm booked solid this weekend."

"Well, it was worth a shot. Maybe some other time."

"Sure, maybe. Thanks for calling, Ed."

"Booked solid" was a major exaggeration. She was meeting a friend—a female friend—for lunch Saturday, then she'd promised to water her mom's plants. The Silver Fox was taking her mother to a golf tournament in Palm Springs.

Was a call from Ed an omen of a bad day, or did it mean her social life was picking up? After all, she didn't refuse dates before nine in the morning very often. Ed wasn't so bad; he just didn't focus well. He had a habit of talking to her and watching other women at the same time.

There was no way to get to work without passing the Big Board. She'd tried not looking in that direction, but she was like an addict needing a daily fix. Every day she discovered something new and endearing about the huge picture of her partner. Certainly this was the first time she'd noticed that wrinkle near his inseam.

"You should have been the one calling," she said to "Giant Joe" as she drove beyond the first of the three billboards. "I can't keep my social life on hold forever while I wait for you to pick up the phone."

Seeing him at work wouldn't count. If he wanted a second date, it was his responsibility to contact her by telephone, even if it meant using the pay phone in the lobby and calling her extension. Maybe this was a teensy bit demanding, but a girl—woman—had to have some standards, even when the whole thing was pretend.

If he'd enjoyed their first date as much as she had, he would have called to say good-night. She arrived at the office mildly disgruntled and afraid her ego was going to take a beating before the dating-etiquette series was finished.

"Good morning." Joe favored her with one of his better smiles, a sample of the open, honest, glad-to-see-you variety.

"Morning." She made a ritual out of stowing her purse in the file, but the sweater could stay where it was. She looked good in her ivory silk tank top and chocolate brown skirt with matching jacket, even though she felt awkward waiting for him to say something about their date. Worse, she had an odd urge to rub up against Joe and purr like a kitten.

"That was fun last night," he said.

Much as she'd hoped he would say something, hearing it in their crowded work space took away some of the luster. He should have called to tell her.

"Yes, it was," she agreed, trying to sound courteous but not too enthusiastic. She was excited about the prospect of a second date, but she had to keep reminding herself it was only part of an assignment. If Joe really wanted to go out with her... But she would be making a serious mistake if she let herself believe that.

"I guess before we get to the column, we should plan our second date. How about tomorrow night?" He made it sound like item number one on his duty roster.

"Sorry, Joe, I'm booked solid this weekend." Ed had bought it. Why not Joe? The least he could do was phone and give her the illusion that it would be a real date.

"Sunday night, too? You can't squeeze me in some time?"

"No."

"I'm picking up something here. Is it because I kept the lavender belle's phone number?"

"Don't be silly. Your social life is your business."

"Then you must be mad because I didn't kiss you good-night."

"That's ridiculous!"

"I did think about it. Give me credit for that."

"I know what's on a man's mind when he gets mushy-faced."

"Mushy-faced!"

She'd scored that time. He sounded genuinely offended.

"We shouldn't be talking about things like this," she said.

"Why not?" His feigned innocence didn't quite cover his irritation.

"If we were really dating, we wouldn't have such personal conversations so soon." She was beginning to wish he would call her from some place far away—say Antarctica.

"Do you mean it's all right for two people to share an intimate evening, but not all right to discuss their feelings? Maybe women's advances over the past twenty-five years have given them a double standard of their own." He was talking fast, like a man on a roll. "Maybe you're planning to take advantage of me on our next date."

"In your dreams!"

"Anticipation is half the fun. I want to know just what's expected of me—and what I can look forward to. If you were disappointed because I didn't kiss you—"

"Of course not!"

"If you were, I'll more than make up for it next time."

"There wouldn't be a second date if I hadn't signed that darn contract," she said, feeling as if a playground bully had just drawn a line in the dirt with a stick.

"I have a column to write," he said in a brusque, businesslike tone.

"So do I," she mumbled, determined to have the last word—preferably in print.

Sunday evening she tried to convince herself the weekend had been busy and productive. She'd cleaned the apartment, done laundry, restocked everything from soup to soap and had lengthy girl chats on the phone with everyone but her friendly neighborhood cosmetics representative. Just to prove she had a life outside the office, she didn't go near the place.

When she did return to work on Monday morning, she learned a whole new meaning of the word "busy." The column debut was a whopping success, and letters were pouring in. They were answering every one, even those with congratulatory messages, but neither had been prepared for the onslaught of questions about dating.

"I'm stumped on this one," Joe admitted, handing her a smudgy letter on lined paper. "How do you tell a ten-year-old girl her boyfriend only wants the homemade cookies in her lunch?"

"Poor kid," Amy said, taking the letter. "She should be winning jump-rope contests or spelling bees, not letting men complicate her life."

"Were you that competitive when you were ten?" Joe asked.

She didn't have an answer.

Not all their letters dealt directly with the column. On Friday she handed Joe an invitation from their old high school.

"They want us to be guests of honor at the spring dance," he said.

"Yes, I read it. What do you think?"

"No reason to refuse. I'll pencil it on my calendar. Want me to answer?"

"No thanks. I will."

He hadn't mentioned their second date again all week, and the lead time for the third installment in the etiquette series was dwindling. If he'd just pick up the phone... But she wasn't going to be the one to bring it up.

That Saturday, a stranger called, an acquaintance of a matchmaking friend. Amy had agreed some weeks ago to go on a blind date with him, but the prospect of spending hours making small talk with a stranger was singularly unappealing. She politely declined, pleading a busy schedule but trying to leave the door open so her friend wouldn't be annoyed.

Amy hadn't set her alarm for Sunday morning, but an irritating noise woke her. She sat up, not pleased to see it was only 7:25. Someone was ringing her doorbell, producing a continual, insistent summons that couldn't be ignored. It must be an emergency! Something had happened to her mother, or the building was on fire.

She bounded out of bed, glanced down at her oversize T-shirt, now faded to a yucky gray-green, and dashed to her closet for a robe. Her old yellow terry bathrobe wasn't much better, but at least it didn't have any embarrassing holes if fire fighters were on the way.

The bell continued its high-pitched droning. Someone was determined to wake her up. If this wasn't a major disaster, somebody had a lot of nerve.

That somebody was Joe Malone. He was standing in the hallway with the thick Sunday edition tucked under his arm and a white paper sack in his hand.

"I thought the place was on fire," she said crossly.

"Good morning to you, too, Patterson. If there had been a fire, your bacon would be crisp by now. I've been out here forever."

"It seemed that way to me, too. You could have called first!"

The man didn't know the three basic rules governing a relationship: phone, phone ahead, and telephone.

He stepped past her into the small living room, looked around at her comfy chintz-covered couch and the thrift-shop tables she'd painted dusty rose to match, and went through to the kitchen.

"Please come in." She closed the door with a bang and followed him to the small round table of her three-piece breakfast set.

"Coffee and doughnuts," he explained unnecessarily as he put down the newspaper and emptied the sack, using a clean plastic plate from her sink drain board to hold at least a dozen assorted high-calorie treats.

"Foam cups are environmentally incorrect," she said, uncomfortably aware of her sleep-tousled hair.

"Sorry, that's all they had at the Gas 'n Go Mart."

He was some classy shopper—supermarket flowers and a convenience-store breakfast.

"It's a little early, Joe. Why are you here?"

"You should ask! After the job you did on me! No wonder you were so secretive about your first dating piece."

"You agreed to do them independently so we wouldn't influence each other."

"That was before you lambasted me for not calling after our first date. I seem to remember asking if we could plan the second."

"If a man wants to see a woman again, he calls. It's so basic I can't believe I'm explaining it."

She stifled a yawn, wishing she hadn't stayed up half the night finishing a mystery novel. She didn't feel up to a debate with Malone.

"We see each other at work every day. There's nothing wrong with asking you for a second date while we're both in the office." He flicked off the plastic lid on one of the cups, took a small sip and passed it to her. "It's hot."

"I told you, office romances don't work. As long as we're pretending to date, we can pretend we don't work together. A phone call was the only way to go."

"What is so special about using the telephone?" He dropped the lid of his cup into the empty bag and put a nutty doughnut on a napkin in front of him.

"It means you made a special effort to get in touch with me—with your date. Setting up personal plans during work hours is too awkward. People are always interrupting us, listening and spreading gossip."

"We share the same little hole in the wall. We're alone together ninety-nine percent of the time. Have a doughnut." He bit into his, and peanut crumbs scattered on the table.

"If you took this seriously, you wouldn't be gobbling doughnuts while we talk."

"I didn't have breakfast. Do you want the other nutty one?"

"No, I like the frosted chocolate."

He put one on a napkin across from where he was sitting. "Sit down. Eat."

"I took the blame for the restaurant snafu. Doesn't that count for something?" she asked, deciding to indulge in the luscious chocolate goody as compensation for being roused from bed to argue with him.

"You made it a bigger deal than it was. Just like your hang-up about needing a phone call."

He was wearing yellow jersey running shorts, which clung to his backside when he went to the sink to add a few drops of water to his coffee.

"Strong stuff," he explained.

"Sure is." She hadn't tasted the coffee yet, but there should be a law against running shorts that left nothing to the imagination. As for the cutoff football warm-up shirt that left his midsection bare, it gave her goose bumps. She had an urge to comb her fingers through the line of fine dark hair that disappeared under the band of his shorts in front.

"You don't like doughnuts?"

"Oh, sure, delicious," she said, taking a bite to show him. What would he think if he could read her mind? He was hard enough to work with without letting him know she'd noticed his buns.

They sat across from each other and ate until the silence between them grew awkward.

"I did say I'd call when I left you Thursday night, didn't I?" He brushed crumbs from the table into his hand, them dropped them into the Gas 'n Go sack.

"Forget I mentioned it."

"No, I've learned my lesson. I'll call you from the lobby of the *Monitor* tomorrow. It will make great column material."

She laughed weakly. It did sound pretty stupid when he said it out loud. "Maybe I went a little overboard expecting you to act like a real date." She couldn't let him think their pretend date had anything to do with her real life.

"Speaking of the column..." He paused to choose another doughnut. "Do you want this one with the little colored things?"

"Sprinkles. No, you take it."

"We haven't done anything about next Sunday's installment. I thought we could do the research by going out today. It's time for our all-day, action-packed second date."

"Where did you come up with that description?"

"From one of those magazines. I accidentally noticed there was an article between a shampoo ad with a nude taking a shower and a panty-hose layout with a topless model. Good thing I decided to read some women's mags to keep tabs on the enemy camp."

"Enemy camp? Is that how you view women?" She licked the last of the chocolate frosting off her fingers.

"Not all women."

"Where do I stand?"

He gave her a long, searching look, reminding her she hadn't combed her hair. "You're more a friend—a good buddy I work with." He seemed relieved to have pegged her.

"So I'm your pal." Next he'd slap her back and ask her to go bowling.

She reached for a blueberry doughnut and took a bite. It felt doughy in her mouth.

"What about today?" he asked.

"Yes, the superdate. I guess it's okay, but I have to wash my car first."

"Is this a new stall—washing your car instead of your hair?"

"My car is so dusty I've forgotten what color it is. Go down and check if you'd like. I'll give you a call when I'm finished."

"Sure, then you'll forget to call."

"Partner, is that distrust I hear? I wouldn't stoop that low."

"I have a better plan. I'll help you, then we can get on with the day's activities."

"That's an offer I might find hard to turn down. I have to haul water from the laundry to the parking lot and—"

"Wait a minute. Why not take it to a car wash?"

"It's a beautiful day. I won't mind a few hours outside."

"Carrying buckets of water?"

"Does sound labor intensive, doesn't it? I'll take it to the car wash and meet you somewhere when it's done."

"Wouldn't it make more sense if we go in the same car? Why don't I take your car to be washed while you get ready. Unless you plan to go as you are."

How awful did she look in the old terry robe? If he hated her sweater... No, it was too hard on her self-esteem to imagine what he thought of her early-morning garb.

"Are you going as you are?" she asked.

"No, I'll change before I come back."

"Into what?"

"Are you asking me what you should wear?"

"It would be helpful if I knew where we're going."

"Just dress casually. Give me your keys."

She found her purse on the kitchen counter and was trying to take the ignition key off the holder without breaking a nail.

"Just give me the bunch."

"I nearly have it off."

"I'm not going to make a copy of your apartment key."

"I suppose not," she admitted, conjuring up a fantasy of Joe naked in her bed, waiting to surprise her—make that *shock* her—when she got home from work some evening. "Tell me where we're going."

He caught the key holder she tossed at him. "It's a surprise."

"Joe..."

"Trust me."

As he left, she checked out all the skin she could see. If he did have a tattoo, it was in a pretty personal place.

"Imagine that," she said to the plastic container she used to store the leftover doughnuts. "A man washing my car."

In all her years of dating, no man had done a favor like that. Some had given her flowers, joke gifts or trinkets. Once she'd even gotten—and returned—a set of lacy black underwear. But no date had ever offered to wash her car. She was extraordinarily pleased. She hated dealing with the hoses and sprays at the do-it-yourself place, and she was always at the wrong angle when she tried to get on track at the automated car wash. In fact, she hated the big brushes. When they swooped down, she always imagined a many-tongued monster swallowing her little car with her inside it.

Joe chose the fastest way to wash her car—he ran it through the automatic. He ordered a hot-wax finish, even though he didn't intend to put anything on his expense account today. It was all right if Amy thought the date was part of their assignment, but he planned to have too much fun to write it off as business.

He didn't take long changing into jeans and a bright yellow-and-white-striped pullover, but the drive back to her apartment seemed like running an obstacle course, thanks to lanes closed for construction. Her car didn't have the zip his did, and he was so eager to start the date that he wanted to get out and push it along faster.

What was the rush? They had all day. Why did he have a nagging suspicion that even a full day together wouldn't be enough time for him to unravel some of the puzzling feelings he had about Patterson?

She opened the door when he got there, obviously ready to go in crisp white walking shorts, white canvas shoes and an orange-brown tank top that complemented her coppery hair. She looked great now, but not even her bulky old bathrobe had turned off his interest.

"You got back fast. What do I owe you for the car wash?"

She slipped into a long-sleeved cotton shirt with funky orange and green dragons chasing each other. He liked looking at her satiny arms and shoulders, but she did have a knack for choosing clothes that suited her.

"In case we're out in the sun," she explained, making him realize he was staring. "I get red even with sunscreen. So how much was it? I have the right change to pay you."

"Not necessary," he said emphatically, refusing when she offered some bills.

"Well, thank you. I really appreciate it. Where are we going?"

"On a mystery trip to places unknown that will haunt your dreams." His imitation of Boris Karloff was corny, but her laughing response pleased him.

Curiosity was her Achilles' heel; she couldn't stand the suspense. She teased him for hints all the way to the fairgrounds, and he had the satisfaction of knowing she was genuinely mystified.

She squealed with delight when she saw the sign: USED BOOK SALE.

"I love to look through old books. Where did you come up with the idea?"

"I made an informed guess. I saw you reading an old hardcover copy of Dorothy L. Sayers's *The Nine Tailors* when you were supposed to be working on a column."

"I only read during my breaks," she protested, her face flushed at the prospect of poring through thousands of old books. "You won't be bored while I look, will you?"

"Not at all. I like to browse, too. I collect books about Arizona history. There's always a chance I might get lucky."

"You should have told me where we were going. I have a canvas bag at home just for book hunting."

"No problem." He pulled out two nylon backpacks and handed her a bright blue one, slipping into a shabby black one himself.

"I can't think of anything more fun than a used book sale," she said, slipping her hand into his as though they walked that way all the time.

He didn't do much book searching himself, only taking a cursory look at a couple of tables when she insisted he not waste the opportunity. Watching her, listening to her excited chatter and tapping into her impressive knowledge of mysteries and authors was even more entertaining than he'd expected.

"Look! A first edition of *Moonspender*. I love Jonathan Gash!"

"Lovejoy." He studied the dust jacket and commented on the good condition, so she wouldn't think he was pretending to be interested in books just to impress her.

There was an odd thought. When had he decided he wanted to impress Patterson?

They left the sale with both backpacks full of bargain books, most of them old mysteries she'd discovered.

"That was a great idea, Joe."

"I haven't lost any points so far?"

"No, it's starting out to be a super action-packed date, but I can't imagine what you have as an encore to book hunting."

He squeezed her hand, surprised by the tingling sensation that rippled up his arm. What was she doing to him?

He tried to remember the frizzy-haired sophomore who'd plagued him in high school, but the appealing woman walking with him blotted out that image.

"Your mystery trip continues," he teased when they got back to the car.

The next leg of their trip seemed incredibly short with Amy by his side.

"You didn't surprise me much this time," she said when they reached the next destination. "I knew we were going to Compadre Stadium when I realized we were heading south toward Chandler."

"Your deductive powers astonish me, madam." His version of Jeremy Brett's Sherlock Holmes wasn't much better than his Karloff, but she stretched her five-and-a-half-foot frame to the max and gave him Watson in return.

"I say, Holmes, what do you expect to learn here?"

"Whether the Cubs have the stuff to whip the Milwaukee Brewers."

"I'll take the Brewers and three runs," she said.

"Don't be silly. There's no point spread in baseball."

"Okay, I'll take the Brewers without points. If they win, you wash my car again."

"And if the Cubs win, you pay a mystery penalty."

"That could be anything! You have to name the stakes."

"I promise it won't cost you more than a car wash."

"Not good enough."

"Forget it. If you don't have confidence in your team . . ."

"Okay, it's a bet."

The stadium was recessed, a cozy bowl with grandstand seating and an area behind the third baseline where families could sit on blankets and lawn chairs. When they arrived, kids were crowding the fence trying to get autographs. Along the outfield wall, people were sitting on top of their RVs to enjoy the game.

"It looks like a sellout," Amy said.

"Yeah, maybe as many as six thousand. I won't lose points for bringing you to a sporting event, will I?" he asked as they seated themselves.

Her smile sent out lightning bolts. "You're already a winner on this date, and the game hasn't even started."

Much to his amusement, he learned she was a yeller. When she wasn't heckling the Cubs, she was shouting advice and encouragement to the Brewers.

"You really want to win this bet," he teased when both teams were scoreless at the bottom of the third.

"If I lose, you might make me do something ridiculous or embarrassing. I want to cancel the bet while they're even."

"No way. A bet's a bet."

"At least tell me what I have to pay."

"You'll have to lose to find out."

He hadn't enjoyed a game so much since he'd pitched a one-hitter in high school. When the Cubs won by one run in the ninth inning, he didn't think a day could be much better.

"Okay, hit me with your worst," she said as they returned to the car.

"Not yet. Part of your penalty is waiting to find out what it is."

"Not fair! I've had enough mystery for one day."

"Have you?" He smiled down at her, wondering how she could look so cute with cherry red cheeks. She was pink wherever the sun had hit her, but he was the one who felt hot. Everything she said and did stoked the fire of his libido, and he had to wonder whether these mock dates were becoming more than he could handle. They were having a wonderful time, but they were still who they were—friendly co-workers. "I'm proud of you," he said. "You didn't take a single note today."

"It's all in zee little gray cells," she said, tapping her head as she quoted Agatha Christie's famous detective.

"I thought we'd end the day with a nice dinner," he suggested when they got back to the city.

"Oh, Joe, after popcorn and hot dogs, I couldn't do it justice."

"Let's just order a pizza, then."

He wasn't happy about the guarded look that came over her face.

"Ordering in may be a little too cozy for a second date."

"Don't let me forget we're on assignment," he said dryly, "but you're off base on this part of the date. Eating pizza in a fully lit living room isn't as intimate as dining over candlelight in a dark restaurant."

"When you put it that way..." She laughed and looked more relaxed.

"Pizza it is."

"My place or yours?" she asked blithely.

"Are we ready for that question yet?" he asked with malicious intent.

"You know what I mean!" She actually managed a noticeable blush in spite of her sunburn. "Where do you want to eat?"

"Your call." They were back in the old mode, negotiating every move. He liked it better when they were just having fun.

"Let's pick up the pizza on the way back to my place. That way you won't have to make an extra trip to take me home."

"You could spend the night on my couch." He tried to sound gallant.

"And go to work in what I'm wearing?"

"Your office mate wouldn't mind."

"Thanks, but no thanks."

* * *

Amy had misgivings about bringing Joe back to her apartment for pizza. It was a nice, normal way to end a perfectly glorious day together, but they weren't a real couple. Maybe it was time to stop playing Cinderella-at-the-ball and start being a columnist on assignment again. The trouble was, she didn't want the day to end yet. Joe had shown her a thoughtful, charming, entertaining, absolutely wonderful side all day.

They waited twenty minutes for their take-out pizza to bake, and for the first time that day, they seemed to have run out of conversation. Amy felt shy with him even though they spent a good chunk of every day in close proximity.

By the time they got back to her apartment, she was edgy and uncomfortable.

"I wonder if we should recommend action-packed, all-day second dates to our readers," she said when they were back in her living room, leaning over the box of sliced double cheese and pepperoni pizza she'd spread out on one of her dusty-rose tables.

"We can talk about it later. Let's consider our date over," he suggested, "and just relax."

"Sounds good to me." She was relieved to know he felt some of the same awkwardness she did.

He picked up her TV remote and flipped through the channels.

"Look what's on the classic movie channel," she said. *"His Girl Friday."*

"One of the good ones," he agreed, leaving the set on that channel.

"I love the style and wit." She caught a long strand of cheese with her tongue.

"Roz Russell was really something."

"I meant Cary Grant."

"He's okay." Joe shrugged.

"Okay! He was dashing, debonair, sophisticated..."

"Is that the kind of man you're looking for?"

"Not exactly, I guess. I've never given it much thought."

"Liar."

"No, I've given a lot of thought to the kind of man I don't want, but not much lately to the kind I do."

"That's reasonable. I apologize for calling you a fibber. What do you look for in a man? I'm just doing some research, of course."

"I thought we were relaxing, not working."

"I'm still curious, but you can drop it if I've hit a sensitive subject."

"Good."

"Good," he echoed less happily.

She could refuse to comment, but she couldn't get Joe's question out of her mind. She liked a man who was pleasant-looking but not necessarily male-model handsome, funny in a kind and caring way, smart, thoughtful—someone who would take her car to be washed. Maybe someone like Joe...but definitely not Joe. He was only—what was his word?—a buddy.

"What are you looking for in a woman?" she asked after they filled several silent minutes by concentrating on the movie and the pizza.

"We tabled that discussion."

"I just wondered. If it's a big deal..."

"No, it isn't with me. I'd like to find a woman who's fun to be with, who enjoys some of the things I like. A sense of humor is important. So are broad interests. I'd rather she didn't talk incessantly, but being too quiet can be a drag. So can asking too many questions."

"Well, I only have one more question for you," she said, not sure whether to take his last dislike personally. "Would you like some ice cream?"

"No, thanks. I don't want to keep you up late. Tomorrow is Monday."

"Watch the rest of the movie, if you like."

"Thanks, but I've seen it at least half a dozen times."

"Those cold Minnesota winters?"

"Something like that. I'll get going now. You've had a long day."

At least he didn't say workday.

"I enjoyed it, Joe. I think we should be positive in the next installment. Emphasize the right things to do on a second date."

"We can talk about it tomorrow."

Why all of a sudden was he so eager to leave? She knew the date was officially over, but...

"We do have one thing pending," he said.

"Oh?"

"You haven't paid your gambling debt."

"Those Cubs! They would win when I wanted them to lose. Any other time..."

"Yeah, it's tough," he said with mock sympathy.

"So what do I owe you?"

"I'm not sure whether I should ask...no, just bake me a cake or something."

"Is that what you had in mind when you made the bet?"

"No, but—"

"I pay my debts. I tried to tell my team how to win, but they insisted on listening to their coach instead of me. I lost, and I owe you."

"I was going to ask for a kiss."

"Oh."

"It's our second date, so..."

"No need to explain." She closed her eyes, hoping he didn't suspect how eager she really was. "I'm ready."

"If I kiss you, it's not for publication."

"That's understood." She opened her eyes; he was still several feet away. "I'm not the type to kiss and tell. Anyway, I wouldn't want anyone to know I bet against the Cubs."

"If you're sure..."

He put his hand on the small of her back and drew her right up against him. She could detect the fresh sunbaked smell of his shirt and the faintly lingering aroma of spicy after-shave. Being in this man's arms was no penalty. She shut her eyes again.

Putting his other arm around her shoulders, he inclined his head, so close now she could feel the tickle of his breath on the tip of her nose. For a panicky instant, she didn't know whether to keep her lips tightly closed or part them slightly.

"You do owe me this," he whispered, letting his lips brush against hers in a touch as light as the whisper of butterfly wings.

"I do," she agreed, forgetting to close her mouth when the words were out.

He lightly stroked one corner of her mouth, then slid his lips over hers to the other.

"Oh." Whatever she'd expected, it wasn't this teasing, ticklish sensation. Even her teeth tingled. "I don't call that a kiss," she whispered breathlessly.

"It isn't. Would you send a pitcher to the mound without a warm-up?"

"Not if I wanted a win," she managed to gasp before his mouth covered hers.

She closed her eyes in time to see stars exploding on the backs of her lids.

Oh, my! she thought. She had to hang on to something for that kind of kiss. She wiggled her hands around his waist just as his mouth engulfed hers.

"Oh, my!" This time she said it aloud when he let her come up for air. "Am I paid up?" She fervently hoped not.

"Paid in full, but since this is our second date—" he kissed her again slowly, making her lips quiver with eagerness ''—I'd be remiss if I didn't kiss you good-night, too,'' he said taking a deep breath.

When he put it that way, she could do only one thing—kiss him back. She puckered her lips against his and could feel their combined efforts all the way to her toes.

''I'd better go,'' he whispered.

Good grief, how did his hand get that low?

''If you say so.'' Was that her voice pretending she didn't care if he went?

''Well, good night.''

He did it again, a softer, sweeter kiss, but no less exciting.

''Thank you.''

''You're the one who's paid a debt.''

''I meant for the day, the book sale, the ball—''

''I know what we did today. Good night, Amy.'' He didn't move away; his lips rested on her Cupid's bow.

''Good night, Joe.''

''Yeah, good night.''

''See you tomorrow.'' At the office. Back in the real world where she didn't date co-workers.

''The way you work, I guess you need your beauty rest,'' he said, backing away from her.

She didn't point out that it wasn't even nine o'clock.

''Well, thanks again for the car wash and—''

''All the other stuff. You've thanked me enough for one night, Patterson.''

He turned to go as if he hadn't shattered their fragile working relationship with his high-powered kisses, then jolted them back to reality by suddenly treating her like a co-worker again. She wanted to give him a swift kick south of his tailbone.

'''Night, Malone.'' Her voice was hoarse only because she'd screamed at the Brewers for nine innings.

7

Amy didn't want to go to work. She shut off the alarm, remembered it was Monday morning and took inventory of her general well-being. She definitely wasn't up to putting in an appearance at the office.

Looking for a reason to stay home, she sniffed loudly but found no cold symptoms; she swallowed but didn't detect a trace of scratchiness. She stretched vigorously, but nothing hurt, not even her minor sunburn.

"Darn it, I feel good," she groused, reluctantly putting her feet on the floor.

No, that wasn't true. She felt like crawling into a hole and hiding. What had made her think she could carry off this pretend-dating stunt with Joe? They'd had too much fun, and his kisses had complicated everything.

How could she work when he made her feel tingly, agitated—aroused? He thought they were only buddies, two people who worked well together. She knew better, and getting involved in an office romance was like living in a house filled with cacti. There was no getting away from the prickers.

"He'll be there ahead of me, waiting to see how his smooching affected me," she muttered to her mirror image. "He'll analyze it, write about it and make me feel like one more notch on his bedpost."

She should warn her female readers: Beware of hot kisses and electric caresses. The lusty guy who could make a woman's senses sing wasn't necessarily looking for love.

She didn't have a clue what Joe wanted, but she didn't like the way their nonrelationship was going.

Now she had a reason to stay home. Thinking about Malone had given her a real headache.

Joe was on his third cup of coffee when he got the message that Patterson had called in sick.

The little chicken, he thought, disappointed because she was almost certainly avoiding him. She was afraid to face him. Just because he'd kissed her, she'd activated her phobia about office romances. If she weren't so obsessed with her job...

That was the kicker. Her job came first. When was he going to meet a woman who could keep a rational perspective on her career?

He thought of calling her, then changed his mind. It wasn't as though they were really forging a personal relationship. They were on assignment. Having a good time together was a plus, but it wasn't crucial.

She was AWOL, out with the blue flu, playing hooky. He didn't for a moment believe anything would keep her home if she wanted to be at the office. It must have been his kiss—kisses—that put her into a tailspin. Maybe his payoff on the bet had been a dumb idea, but he'd learned one thing—she kissed back. Did she ever!

He had enough to do without worrying about his partner. Why couldn't he concentrate on something besides plans for dates number three, four and five? The last thing he wanted was involvement with a woman who was more interested in her job than in a relationship. She had made it clear from the beginning that dating co-workers was off-limits for her.

The day dragged, but it had nothing to do with missing her.

He came to work Tuesday morning with a plan. If Patterson didn't show up for work, he was going to make a house call at her apartment. Maybe she did need chicken soup and TLC; more likely she was malingering. She was either going to work or to a doctor to be checked over. If necessary, he would take her temperature to decide which it was. He was relishing the role he'd assigned himself when he walked into the office and found her already at the computer.

"Well, you're back." So much for his fantasy of playing doctor. "What was wrong with you?"

"Just a little under the weather."

"My grandfather gets 'under the weather.' You need a better excuse than that."

"Could be I got too much sun."

"You don't need to kid me, Patterson. I'm not the truant officer around here."

"I'm not on the clock," she said defensively. "All I have to do is produce my half of the column."

"What about sending out responses, doing publicity, finishing the dating series—"

"You have no reason to complain. I do my share."

She was too comfortable when she could talk about work. He wanted her to squirm a little more.

"I think you were faking." He perched on the edge of the desk so he could look down on her. "You were scared to come in because of what happened after the sun went down."

"You're delusional!"

"You thought I might corner you in the supply room or chase you around the watercooler."

"Be serious, Joe. I have work to do."

"Isn't that why you're afraid to date co-workers? You had an experience with some nasty reporter who pinched your fanny behind the file cabinet or—"

"If you think you're funny, think again!"

"I'm only trying to understand why you're so paranoid about dating men you work with—me, for instance."

"I have the right to choose whom I see socially."

"Sure, and our dates are all business. You were doing research when you kissed me."

"*I* kissed *you!* If that bet wasn't a juvenile ploy, I've never seen one. *You* kissed *me!*"

"And a sweet bit o' puckering you did, too, me dear," he said in a pseudo-Irish accent.

"Oh, stop it!"

"It seems you left your sense of humor at home."

"Unlike you, I come here to work."

"To catch up." He knew he was belaboring the point, but she was affecting him like an itch in a place he couldn't reach to scratch.

At that moment, Bertram Garver made an entrance, clearing his throat to get the respectful silence he thought he deserved. "Joe, Amy, I'd like to congratulate you. The column is going well—as I thought it would—and the series on dating etiquette looks like a smash hit. The publisher loves it. He called me himself to make sure you can stretch it into at least eight installments. We'll talk later about a topic for your next Sunday series. It's premature to talk syndication, but keep up the good work."

"Thank you, Mr. Garver," Amy said, "but I'm afraid the dating series will get stale if we try to—"

"See that it doesn't," he said brusquely, doing an about-face and marching out of their cubicle.

"You could have said something," she said, standing to confront Joe. "We can't possibly do eight pieces."

"Do you think two dates are enough to cement a relationship?"

"Of course not, but—"

"Do you want to tell our esteemed publisher, William III, he's backing a pair of losers?"

"We're not losers! And we're not a pair, either."

"We are until we wrap up the dating series. Planning our next date will have to be top priority."

"We can wing it—make something up."

He shook his head with mock solemnity.

"Nothing is going to happen on our dates that hasn't already happened," she insisted.

"Maybe not, but we'd better figure out what dating ground we haven't covered. We have to come up with a fresh idea."

"I can't do anything Saturday. I'm going to a wedding."

"There you are! Perfect fodder for the series. I'll go with you."

"You aren't invited."

"Don't try to tell me you can't bring an escort. I've never gotten a wedding invitation that didn't include a guest of my choice."

"I suppose I could take you," she grudgingly conceded, "but why would I want to?"

"Use your head, Patterson. What's more stressful than watching another bachelor take the fall?"

"For you maybe. I love weddings."

"They give women ideas. If a couple is just starting to date—"

"He might be scared off if he thinks she's imagining him as a groom."

"Admit it has possibilities—unless you have a better idea. We have to do something before next Monday to fill our column inches."

"Oh, all right. Three o'clock in Scottsdale. I cry at weddings, and champagne makes me silly. I'll only bring you if you agree to show me what you write before it goes into the paper.''

"I'll feel a lot safer if I can preview your stuff, too.''

"Then we have a deal—a business deal.''

"Fine with me.''

Amy thought about calling in sick every day for the rest of the week. She didn't. What she did was worse. She worried about anything and everything. She couldn't seem to decide what to wear to work. She fretted if her hair was too frizzy or too straight. She tried a new shade of lipstick and a darker eye shadow and hated both.

Worse, she didn't feel like an equal partner in the column anymore. Something was awry in her dealings with Joe. By Friday she admitted the truth to herself. She was behaving like a woman involved in a personal relationship with a co-worker. She didn't like it.

There was only one way to get back on track: Joe had to accept that they were only fulfilling an assignment when they went out together. That meant no holding hands, no flirting and certainly no kisses. Just to be sure he got the message, she decided to put her apartment off-limits.

"When should I pick you up tomorrow?" he asked Friday afternoon.

"Oh, don't bother. I need to come in for a little while tomorrow. Just pick me up outside the building at two.''

He gave her his skeptical, arched-eyebrow look but didn't argue. "Yes, ma'am, I'll be there.''

That evening, she tried on every dress she owned, even the one on the billboard, but her wardrobe was woefully inadequate when it came to spring weddings. She settled on an old reliable navy with buttons down the front and a full, sweeping skirt. A pattern of creeping vines saved it from being matronly, but she wasn't thrilled with it.

She woke up Saturday morning knowing the navy dress wouldn't do. She hit the mall.

Her favorite shop had a dozen dresses that were perfect—for the mother of the bride. She dashed from store to store, rejecting lace, satin, silk, filmy net and everything else that swirled, shone or clung. She absolutely couldn't wear a dress that would make Joe think she was trying to dazzle him.

Time was running short when she dashed into a trendy boutique that made her clothing budget look like petty cash. Almost ready to wear her practical navy, she flipped through dresses on a sale rack. It was love at first sight! She rushed to a changing room and slipped into a bare-shouldered peach cotton-blend dress with more oomph than the average bikini. It was short; she'd have to remember not to tug at the hem. It was sexy; narrow straps crisscrossed in front leaving a little hidey-hole bare between her breasts. It fitted like a second skin, but best of all, it made her look sensational without any frills to make Joe think she'd combed a dozen shops in search of the perfect dress.

Even if the dress was on sale, the price tag was outrageous, but she didn't bother to calculate how many months that charge would ride on her credit card balance.

Practically breathless from hurrying, she managed to buy a pair of dressy sandals with outrageously high heels and a delicate little purse with a long, narrow shoulder strap.

Fate was on her side. She walked into a no-appointment beauty salon and in only a few minutes had her hair hanging over a sink. In less than forty-five, she walked out with a becoming upswept hairstyle, but one that didn't involve too drastic a change from her everyday look.

"Eat your heart out, Malone," she muttered as she lugged her purchases to the car.

She got back to the apartment with everything she needed but time. Her stomach was twisted in knots, but no matter how fast she hurried, she wasn't going to make it to the office on time to meet Joe.

"It was silly posturing, making him meet me there," she told her phone receiver as she frantically checked for his number, then remembered it wouldn't be in the directory. She had to call information because he had a new listing.

She'd overlooked the obvious way to keep him from coming to her apartment.

"Joe," she said, her heart still racing when he answered, "it's me—"

"Me?" he interrupted.

"Amy." As if he didn't know. "I'm running a little late. I'll pick you up, since it's on the way to Scottsdale."

"No need. I'll come by your apartment. It's not a problem."

She didn't have time to argue, not if she wanted to watch her friend walk down the aisle. If she really hurried, she could meet him down on the pavement.

The doorbell rang just as she was putting on the final touch, her pearl-drop earrings.

His expression made her financially ruinous shopping spree worthwhile.

"You look terrific." He was practically speechless.

"Thanks. So do you." She tried to sound offhanded, casual, as if she got compliments like that every day.

"I mean it. That dress should be on the billboard."

Right, Joe. Remind me of the Big Board. Ruin my day. She stifled this rejoinder and hustled him out the door.

Even though this was another pretend date with her writing partner, she felt like a prom queen as she carefully walked to the car in her slippery-soled new spike heels. Joe looked as if he'd made a special effort, too. He was wearing a suit the color of old ivory, with a linen shirt and a dark brown tie patterned with tiny ivory chess knights.

Either his boots were new or he'd spent a lot of time polishing them to a honey brown sheen.

Wouldn't we have made a good couple at his senior prom? she thought. But, of course, Joe Malone wouldn't have taken her to a demolition derby in high school. It was crazy to compare this pseudodate to a school dance, but their invitation to the spring formal had brought back memories of the ones she'd missed.

"Who's getting married?" he asked as they drove toward Scottsdale.

"Cindy Weller. We've known each other since fourth grade. You probably know her, too. She was on the varsity cheerleading squad for three years."

"I don't remember her."

"Tall, blond, famous legs. You knocked her down once when you ran out of bounds at a football game."

"I draw a blank on that, too."

"You're sure to recognize her. I shouldn't tell you, but it's ancient history now. She had a major crush on you. She practically stalked you for months."

"You're making this up."

"Like my mission in life is to pump up your ego?"

"And the groom—what does he do?"

"He's an anesthesiologist. You have the typical male mind-set, Malone. You asked what the groom does, but it never occurred to you that the bride might have an interesting profession, too."

"Does she?"

"Sort of. She's a systems analyst for the Erikson Corporation."

"What does a systems analyst do?"

"Analyzes systems, I guess."

"You don't have a clue, either."

* * *

When they arrived at the church, other guests were ahead of them waiting to be seated by ushers in midnight blue tuxes.

The golden oak pews in the spacious modern nave were already half-filled, but Joe noted with relief that the interior of the church was pleasantly cool. He didn't see any familiar faces, and darned if he could remember knocking over some leggy blond cheerleader when he played quarterback on the high school team. It was considerably more puzzling that he remembered so much about Amy, pest that she was in those days. He could still see her wearing a big, sloppy, men's dress shirt, probably filched from her father's closet, and tight jeans that strained at the seams. She'd emerged out of her chubby cocoon with the splendor of a butterfly. In some odd way, knowing how much she'd changed made her even more appealing.

"I still can't believe you don't remember Cindy."

"Believe it."

She still had the tenacity of a pit bull with a bone when she got an idea in her head. That hadn't changed since the first time he'd seen her, a meeting impressed on his mind because she'd knocked his lunch tray out of his hands when they collided. Someday, she was going to push him too far, and . . .

"Friends of the bride or groom?" a young usher asked in a hushed voice more appropriate for a funeral than a wedding.

Joe followed a few steps behind Amy and the usher, fascinated by her provocative walk. Her heels were too high. She'd be lucky if she didn't break one off and tip over, but he did appreciate the way they accentuated her slender ankles and sleek calves.

He took his place beside her and glanced at the program. The best thing about this wedding was that he wasn't in it. The memory of rented tuxes that didn't allow for arm

movements and formal shoes that pinched like a vise were
only too vivid. How many friends had he helped take the
big step?

"Seven bridesmaids," Amy whispered. "Thank heav-
ens she has lots of sisters and cousins and didn't ask me.
For a while, I kept a consignment resale shop supplied with
taffeta and satin."

"I thought you loved weddings."

"It's starting," she said, shushing him as all the spectators stood.

The parade of bridesmaids began with a matronly brunette in a silvery gray dress that billowed out well below her
knees. Instead of sleeves, the dresses had big bunches of
netting at the shoulders.

"They look like bat wings," Joe whispered.

Amy giggled without looking at him.

"Smart bride," he commented.

"Someone will hear you!"

It seemed unlikely; the organ was loud enough to make
the stained-glass windows vibrate.

Her curiosity got the best of her. "Why is she smart?
Because she had a crush on you?" She moved closer so he
could hear her whisper.

"No, those bridesmaid dresses guarantee she'll be the
prettiest one in the wedding party."

"You're terrible!"

She was amused, not angry. For some reason, that
pleased him immensely. He held back his next witty comment because the bride was starting down the aisle doing
the hesitation two-step, clutching the arm of a pudgy,
balding man who seemed to be suffering from rented-tux
syndrome. Or maybe he was tallying up the bills.

Her dress had kept some sweatshop workers busy for
days. The top had enough little pearls to add three inches
to an already impressive bustline. Why did a woman think
she needed a hundred yards of material bunching out from

her waist to the floor and down the aisle to make an impression? Patterson was the one who was going to turn heads at the reception. She looked fantastic in a little piece of cloth too small to polish his car.

"My ten bucks against any stake you choose says that thing on her head will fall off before she says 'I do,'" he whispered.

"You are really awful!" She couldn't suppress a small grin.

"But am I on?"

"Okay, if you'll be quiet!"

When the bride had been handed over to the tall, foxy-faced groom, the crowd sat.

"Are those shoes comfortable?" Joe quickly asked before the minister began talking.

"Perfectly."

It would add immeasurably to his enjoyment of the ceremony if she would put her feet on his lap. The heels looked dangerous, but stroking the ankles was worth the risk. A man needed a few fantasies in situations like this.

Assorted friends and relatives read and sang. They were getting down to the business of making joint tax returns legal when he glanced at Amy. She had a tiny pad of paper on her lap and was secretly making notes with a pencil stub.

He rolled his eyes, and she got the message.

"I'm only capturing the ambience," she whispered, but she put her notes away.

After the ceremony, a pair of self-important young ushers dismissed the guests row by row beginning at the front. As latecomers, Joe and Amy were so far back his seat was numb before they finally got the nod to leave.

Joe hated reception lines. This one formed right outside the church door, making escape impossible. He kissed the bride he still didn't remember, congratulated the groom, who had the usual goofy expression on his face, and introduced himself to parents, grandparents and bridesmaids. The word that they were the billboard couple spread down the line to the bat-winged female attendants. Ordinarily he might enjoy a little fawning, a few squeals of excitement. Patterson's stoic expression made him eager to get away.

"Let's go," he said, putting his hand on her waist and propelling her out into the bright afternoon sun. "Want to skip the reception?" he asked.

"No."

"No harm asking."

"You wouldn't be you if you didn't try to wiggle out of it," she said.

Amy read the directions sent with the invitation, and Joe drove to the swanky hotel where the reception was being held. The Gatemore had valet parking, so he surrendered his key with a jaundiced look at the ponytailed, red-coated attendant.

"Don't block it. We probably won't stay long."

"You're in a party mood," she chided dryly.

"We are here on business, aren't we?"

"You are. I can get a ride home if you get bored."

He grunted, but she didn't know if he was agreeing or disagreeing.

Buffet tables flanked the outdoor pool, reminding Amy that breakfast was only a distant memory and she hadn't had a bite for lunch. She didn't even know if her new dress allowed room for eating.

Joe wasn't a shy guest who hung back from the food. He led her to a table of canapés and was the first to dig into a display of fresh shrimp arranged on a heart-shaped platter. She didn't need too much urging to fill a plate with carrot curls, stuffed celery and hot puff pastries, the most recognizable appetizers in the array of fancy finger foods.

On a separate table, a champagne fountain dispensed pink bubbly. Joe filled a goblet for both of them, and they sipped, nibbled and wandered.

Exotic tropical fish swam in miniaquariums on the dining tables. The cake was a five-tier confection adorned with white sugar roses and delicate green leaves.

"If you were taking notes—don't start, this is a hypothetical question—but if you were, what would you find noteworthy about this reception?" Joe asked.

"It's pretty lavish. Imagine how much work went into cutting out all those fancy sandwich shapes, for example—and I understand this is only the first course. They'll bring out the real banquet later."

"I don't think our readers will be thrilled by a menu, even if there is enough here to feed all the players in the NFL for a month. Datewise, what are you picking up?"

"Probably the same things you are."

"You're coming up empty, too!" He sounded triumphant. "I'd a hell of a lot rather be someplace alone with you—with my date."

"We don't have to give this outing a thumbs-up rating. Maybe weddings are poor places to take a date, especially early in the relationship. Let's go look at the presents."

"They'll need a moving van to haul this home," Joe said gloomily as they circled a long table piled high with unwrapped gifts. "There's enough wrapping paper here to cover a 747."

"You do for weddings what Scrooge did for Christmas," she complained. "Lighten up, Joe. This is Cindy's day of days."

"The groom's, too." He nodded toward a man with his arm draped around a shapely redhead with bat sleeves.

"He's coming on to a bridesmaid," Amy said indignantly. "That rat!"

"What did we give the happy couple? Hope you didn't spend too much. I give them six months."

"A china serving bowl. I didn't sign your name."

"We came together. Shouldn't we give a gift together? Point of etiquette. Maybe we can find your package and add my name to the card," he suggested.

"Even if you were serious—and I know you're not—two dates don't make us a couple. Anyway, I had the gift delivered ahead of time."

"I think bringing me to a wedding escalates the relationship. It's a more serious date than going to a stock car race or a country line dance."

"Is that what you have in mind to get this series over with?"

"Only two of many suggestions. In fact, we could leave now and go to—"

"You can leave any time. I'm staying until they cut the cake." She found a place to put her empty plate and goblet.

"Maybe things will pick up. Look."

A short distance beyond the pool area a band was warming up on a big veranda.

"Classy." She watched four musicians in white dinner jackets begin to play.

Joe grinned and pulled her by the hand.

"What are you doing?"

"That's a dancing tune, lady."

"But shouldn't the bride and groom begin—"

"Do you see a bride? Do you see a groom doting on his new wife? Let's have fun!"

"I don't think—"

"That's 'Blue Moon.' Big band stuff." He started humming with the music.

"I didn't know you like the oldies."

"Honey, there's a whole lot you don't know about me. Let's go. Didn't your mommy teach you it's bad manners to keep a gentleman waiting?"

They were the first ones to begin swaying to the music, but others soon followed their lead.

"This could turn out to be a fine wedding," he said, leading her through some unfamiliar steps and leaning forward so his cheek was against her upswept hair.

"You're really good—at dancing," she said a little breathlessly.

He was a strong leader, guiding her with his hand flat on the small of her back.

"They used to call this necking to music." He hummed some more, caressing her earlobe with his lips as the melodic notes flowed all the way to her toes. "Tell me," he said, "when the bride walked down the aisle, did you imagine yourself in her place?"

"Well, no, not exactly."

"Be honest. I'm trying to understand why women get so wrapped up in weddings."

He was holding her so close it was hard to concentrate. She could feel the warmth of his back where her hand rested on his jacket, and it was hard not to imagine the smooth, muscular contours of his torso.

"They're just romantic."

"Not much of an explanation." He dropped his other hand to her waist, so she was left swaying between his arms, her cheek resting against his chest.

"Romance is the difference between candles you use when the lights go out and white tapers in silver holders— the ingredient that makes a ball gown shimmer with magic while the same material in a show girl's costume is gaudy."

"Next you'll make me believe in fairy dust and love potions." He said it without mockery, not releasing her even though the music had stopped.

"Well . . ." She tried to back away, but he didn't show any indication that he'd release her. "The music stopped."

"I know," he said. "I'm just trying to get a handle on what goes on in your head."

"Should I tell you all about myself in twenty-five words or less?"

"No, I'm more than willing to hear the equivalent of *War and Peace* on tape."

"There's not that much to tell."

"The wise and sharp-witted columnist—is she the person you go to sleep as at night?"

"I don't know how to answer that."

"You're complicated."

"No, everyone has different facets to their personality. You, for instance."

"No, the subject is you."

"We're standing here alone. All the other dancers have left."

"Hard to believe we danced through a whole set." He tilted up her chin and studied her face.

"We didn't. The bride and groom must be doing something."

"Let them do whatever they like."

"That zero! Why did she pick him?"

"Love is blind?"

"There's a column idea."

"No column ideas now. I'm tired of being held at arm's length by Amy Patterson, girl reporter. Your job obsession—is it just your way of hiding what you really are?"

"What am I really?" *Uncomfortable, for one thing!* Maybe she didn't know as much as she thought she did about Joe Malone.

"That's what I've decided to find out."

He had that mushy look, but she knew he wasn't going to kiss her. This wasn't about kissing. She could handle kissing.

"Tell you what," he said softly, dropping his hands another inch, dangerously close to fondling her bottom. "Let's have some more champagne."

"It makes me—"

"I know, but I have a feeling a silly Amy might be a lot of fun."

"I think I'll duck inside—look for the powder room." She needed to splash cold water on her face, do deep-breathing exercises. She'd definitely lost control of their conversation, and losing control was what threatened her most about working with Joe. He was always so confident, so poised, so self-possessed, so damned-macho-cocksure together!

"Don't forget to come back," he called after her.

Did he read minds, too?

She met an old friend on the way into the hotel, then another in the powder room. By the time she went back outside, she'd had a few flashes of inspiration about Joe's odd behavior. He could be baiting her, hoping for some juicy tidbits to write about. Or maybe he needed to intimidate her to preserve his self-esteem.

Or maybe she was bogged down in professional rivalry or the kind of psychobabble she usually avoided.

What was going on with the two of them? Now that she'd regained her composure, she was eager to continue their probing conversation.

Joe wasn't hanging around the veranda or the champagne fountain. She helped herself to a small squirt of bubbly and sipped it while she looked for him. Of course, it was possible he'd taken her up on her earlier offer to find her own ride home. She had been gone a long time. Wouldn't that make a good point on dating etiquette? Is it ever proper to abandon the person you came with?

No, Joe wouldn't do that, not without telling her. She hoped. Because if he had, she would have to draw and quarter him in the next installment of the series, and that wasn't how she was feeling toward him right now.

She wandered, talking to several people, until she spotted him beside the pool. He was standing so close to the water it was a wonder he wasn't worried about getting splashed.

Amy got closer, and it was obvious why his mind wasn't on his outfit. He was having an animated conversation with a shapely brunette—either someone who was staying at the hotel or a wedding guest who'd thought to bring a chartreuse bikini to the reception. Now there was a column topic: what to do when your date deserts you for another woman.

"Amy!" He spotted her and motioned her to come over. "You remember Dana DeJong."

"Of course, the morning show." In a half hour of sizzling conversation, Amy had managed to interject two sentences—no, make that phrases—in their interview. DeJong hadn't pretended to be interviewing anyone but "Giant Joe" himself.

"You remember my co-worker, Amy Patterson."

"Hello. Now, Joe, you can't tell me..."

Amy was in jeopardy the moment she stepped onto the side of the pool. The wet concrete was slippery, especially on the smooth leather soles of her brand-new shoes. She belatedly decided to retreat, but her legs separated, propelling one foot toward the aquamarine depths of the pool and the other toward a shallow, water-filled indentation in the paving.

She reached for Joe and shrieked; at the same moment she did the splits. He tried to grab her but swung his arm across her shoulders instead of catching her arm. The collision destroyed the last of her balance, and she plunged headfirst into the chlorinated water.

Before she could surface, he was in the water, diving down to rescue her.

"Oh, Joe!" She popped up, either crying or laughing, not sure which.

His boots were a far cry from diving fins. He got his head above water, but for an instant she thought he might need saving himself.

"We're all wet!" she cried out.

"Oh, baby, leave it to you to sum up a situation!"

A moment later, they were hauling themselves over the edge of the pool, grasping at strange hands extended to help them. The waiters must have practiced for such an emergency; they surrounded them with towels, and the hotel manager rushed up more quickly than an ambulance chaser could say "lawsuit."

"We're fine," Joe assured everyone, putting his arm around her and trying to get away without further loss of dignity.

The party was over for them, and Amy belatedly wondered if her new dress was washable.

8

Familiar faces materialized out of nowhere. Amy could have sworn she didn't know more than a dozen people at the reception, but, wet to the skin with her hair a soggy mess, she had to run a gauntlet of old school friends when they left the pool area.

"Too much champagne," she heard someone say, but most of the buzzing was sympathetic—or curious.

"I didn't know you and Joe were really an item. I thought the billboards were only, you know, publicity."

Amy vaguely remembered the gossip-hungry woman who fell in beside her as the girl in chem class who held the school record for broken test tubes.

"We work together. That's all," Joe said, his arm around her shoulders as they tried to make their escape.

Amy wasn't as pleased hearing it from him as she would have been saying it herself.

They lost their spectators when they rounded the last corner on their dash to the car. Joe extracted a soggy parking stub from his jacket pocket and handed it to the same kid who'd parked it, then they looked at each other and started laughing.

Even the bill he extracted from his money clip to tip the valet was damp. He waved it in the air to dry it, and Amy thought he was funnier than a comedy club headliner. Still laughing at him, she pulled the pins from her hair and tried to dry it by shaking her head the way dogs did to dry their fur. He doubled over laughing.

"Are we hysterical?" she gasped between gales of laughter.

"Probably." He made a mock-heroic effort to get serious, but it only set her off again.

"Your car, sir." The kid with the ponytail backed away from them so quickly Joe had to pursue him to hand over the tip.

"He thinks we're lunatics." Amy giggled as Joe went through the door-opening ceremony with exaggerated gestures.

"A sense of humor isn't a prerequisite for parking cars."

They sat in the no-parking zone for a minute and caught their breath before driving away.

"I really am sorry," he said when they couldn't laugh anymore.

"It wasn't your fault."

"I tried to catch you and instead knocked you into the pool."

"I slipped on the wet concrete. I was already headed in that direction."

"Your shoes—"

"I know! The heels were too high, and I didn't even bother to scrape the soles with sandpaper so they wouldn't be so slippery."

"You bought new shoes for our date?"

"Don't make too much of it! I needed them."

"You needed shoes that make walking on stilts look easy?"

She bent and loosened the tight straps across the tops of her feet and wiggled her toes in relief.

"Don't you ever buy something new just because you're going someplace?" she asked.

"Sure, I got the charcoal suit for our dinner date."

"Did you really? That's so sweet, Joe."

"I can use it as an interview suit if we drop the ball on the column."

"Thanks a lot! Talk about turning a compliment into an insult!"

"I didn't mean it that way. I think the column is going to fly." He drove away from the curb. "By the way, you looked terrific today."

"How do you like the water-soaked look? Do you think I'll start a new trend?"

"Sarcasm from you? How unusual. Is that a new bra, too?"

She looked down, remembering too late that the dress came with a built-in foundation. She wasn't wearing a bra, but the wet cloth wasn't much better than cellophane for concealing the hard points of her nipples. He got her that time!

"Everyone saw!" She crossed her arms over her chest. "I didn't realize—oh, darn!"

"Don't worry. I think you're one of those rare women who look better without clothes than with them."

"You don't know that!"

"I'd like to." He said it with such quiet conviction she decided to drop the subject of her public humiliation.

"I hope your suit isn't ruined. You looked nice today."

Truth to tell, he was so wet she knew he was wearing Jockey shorts with a paisley print.

"Should we write about disastrous wedding dates?" he asked.

She shrugged. "I guess."

"Just guess? Don't you want to rehash the details, point out my shortcomings as an escort?"

"No."

"Why not?"

"I don't want to think about it anymore today."

Fortunately, he seemed to be paying attention to where they were going. Her mind was so muddled they might end up south of the border if he depended on her for directions.

"You're shivering. It's hotter outside than in here. I'd better turn the air off and open the windows."

"What?" she asked in mock horror. "And let the wind mess my hair?"

"Don't! I can't laugh anymore. My ribs ache."

"I wish it was dark." She squinted because her soggy little purse was too small to hold sunglasses, and the late afternoon sun was still bright enough to turn car windows on the highway into blinding glares.

"Because you don't want your neighbors to see you coming home wet? No problem. My place is closer anyway. We'll stop and get some dry clothes before I drive you home."

"Thanks, but I think I'd rather go straight to my apartment."

"I'm going to need gas to get back home from your place. Darned if I'll get out in a soaking wet suit to pump it."

"Running out of gas! That's an excuse I never expected to hear in this lifetime. I'll just wait in the car while you change."

"You can come in long enough for me to change without compromising your reputation or whatever it is you're worried about," he said coolly. "But if you're nice, I'll lend you something dry."

"What? Castoffs left behind by your old girlfriends?"

"Generally speaking, they don't leave street wear behind, but I'll find something. Unless you're afraid of me."

"Oh, boy," she muttered under her breath. The pretend dates were getting more complicated every time they tried one.

His apartment complex was a two-story tan stucco with small balconies on the upper floor.

"Do you live upstairs or down?" she asked.

"Both. Every unit has a living room and kitchen down and two bedrooms up. I use one as a home office for my desk and computer."

The parking lot had a scattering of cars but no people in sight. Unless he had neighbors who hid behind their curtains with binoculars, she should be able to dash inside without anyone seeing her soggy condition.

His living room was sparsely furnished, but everything in sight showed marvelous taste: a pine trunk with brass-plated hardware served as a coffee table, and a smaller, similar one was used as an end table next to a suede-seated rocking chair. A futon cushion that could roll out into a bed had a colorful motif of russet, teal and pale orange triangles in a distinctive Southwestern pattern. An oak bookcase was filled to capacity with old volumes, most without dust jackets, probably his Arizona history collection. This was the first time she'd seen the utilitarian beige carpeting so popular with landlords really look like part of the decor.

"This is a great room, Joe—peaceful and inviting."

"Were you expecting neon beer signs and pinups?" he teased but looked pleased by her compliment.

He'd left the air-conditioning set on a cool temperature because it was unseasonably hot for April, and she was still damp enough to shiver.

"Why don't you go up and rinse the chlorine off in the shower? Give me a chance to get out of my wet clothes and find something for you to wear."

"Would you mind? I smell like a locker room."

To his credit, he didn't make any jokes about her ill-fated locker room crusade.

It was odd being in his bathroom, knowing this was where he did all the personal things that made him look so great. The whole room had pale blue tile wainscoting, the same kind that lined the area around the tub/shower. The upper walls and ceiling had rough, grainy plaster painted stark white. The window and shower curtains had a design of blue marine life. He kept a vivid royal blue bath rug beside the tub and one towel that matched it on a bar. The towel looked used, so she opened a built-in cupboard and found another, fluffy and neatly folded on a paper-lined shelf.

Compared to her brothers, he was Mr. Neat. Everything in the place was clean enough to make it look as if he'd been expecting company.

Did he think . . . ? No, he couldn't possibly have anticipated that she might end up here. No way! Impossible! She'd never given him the slightest encouragement. Had she?

She peeled off her dress and panty hose, but couldn't resist one temptation—peeking into the medicine cabinet over the sink. He used menthol shaving cream, injector razor blades, two kinds of expensive after-shave, stick deodorant and dental floss. His toothpaste and a red toothbrush were in a holder on the sink counter.

"No secrets there." She stripped off her wet pink panties and stepped out of the sausagelike roll they made around her feet, then dropped them on the pile she'd made of her other clothing. She hoped she hadn't ruined a dress that wasn't even paid for.

Just to justify a little more snooping, she decided he wouldn't begrudge her a dollop of shampoo. Her hair was going to be frizzy when it dried; it might as well be clean and frizzy.

She found it necessary to check all the cupboards, none of which contained anything the least bit interesting. Still, it was worth looking. She'd discovered her aunt's secret hoard of sex manuals that way when she was still in grade school. Unfortunately, she'd gotten caught before she had a chance to read much. When she didn't find any shampoo, she checked the shower. A nearly full bottle was on the soap ledge, just where she kept hers.

When she stepped under the water, her imagination started working overtime. Maybe she should use cold! She was enjoying the needles of warm water that pelted her skin much more than anyone should enjoy a stranger's shower. And she definitely shouldn't be fantasizing about the man who usually stood where she was. She could visualize his body pummeled by water jets until he was pink and glowing, his dark hair soaked but curly on his broad, hard chest, water cascading down his flat stomach....

She shouldn't be having these thoughts! She shampooed and rinsed with all possible haste and climbed out of the tub to towel off.

"He can't possibly look as good as I imagine him," she told the digital scale when she stepped on it, putting aside the damp towel she'd just used so it wouldn't add to her weight. "One fourteen. I like your scale better than mine, Malone."

She nearly fell off when he knocked on the door.

"Open the door a crack, and I'll hand you some clothes," he said.

"Just a minute!"

She had a sudden attack of modesty bordering on panic, possibly triggered by guilt about her shower fantasies. A woman should make up men to dream about, not use real live ones that came knocking on the door. She grabbed the damp towel and wound it around herself sarong-style.

Covered as she was, she still opened the door only enough to stick one bare arm out to grab the bundle he offered.

"Thanks."

"No problem. If those don't work, I'll look for something else."

A few minutes later, she came downstairs wearing black sweatpants and a matching sweatshirt with sleeves rolled up so her hands could hang out. It felt odd not to be wearing underwear, but it wasn't visually obvious.

"Get something to drink in the fridge," Joe called down from unseen heights. "I'm going to shower."

Considering how often she'd been immersed in water that day, she felt surprisingly dehydrated. She took him up on his offer and found a diet lemon-lime soda. The glasses in his cupboard were arranged in military rows, sorted by size. The matched set made her odds and ends look like garage-sale leftovers. She filled one with ice cubes, the only thing he kept in his freezer compartment. They did have something in common.

She poured her drink with ceremonial slowness, concentrating on the crackling ice and bubbles rising in the glass. Joe undoubtedly took showers with regularity, but she'd never visualized the process before. Just because he was taking one virtually over her head didn't mean she had to fantasize. . . .

She took a big swallow of her drink, and bubbles went up her nose. How much more would her dignity suffer today?

When Joe came down, she was sitting at his scrubbed pine kitchen table holding her glass so it wouldn't leave a wet stain.

No fair, Joe! she wanted to say. He was wearing nothing but shorts, gray knit shorts, the soft, clingy kind that showed without a doubt he was a male of the species. She couldn't look at him because, if she accidentally dropped her eyes below his waist, he was sure to think she was checking him out.

He found a soda for himself, and she took a quick look when he tipped his head back to drink from the can. Oh, wow! It was time to go home. Was it ever!

"Did my medicine cabinet pass muster?"

"What makes you think . . . ?" She was going to have to practice sounding indignant.

"Someday your obsessive curiosity is going to get you in trouble." He was grinning. "But not today. How about a sandwich?"

He opened the fridge; she noticed the bananas, a huge bunch large enough to keep a family of chimps happy.

"What I really need is a plastic bag for my soggy clothes and a ride home."

"I've already folded your clothes and put them in a bag."

"Thanks." She got goose bumps thinking of Joe unrolling her briefs and neatly folding them.

"Is our official date over?" he asked, breaking off two bananas and handing one to her.

She peeled it to give her hands something to do. He stripped the thick yellow skin off his and took a big bite.

She nibbled at the banana to give herself time to think. He finished his and took away her glass and peel.

"There is one thing I want to know first," she said.

Why was he smiling at her that way? The look in his eyes was enough to turn the rest of her banana to mush.

"What's that?"

"Do you really have a tattoo?"

"Yes, I do."

"Well..."

"Well?"

"Where is it?"

"Do you want to see it?"

"Yes—no."

"Which is it?"

He put his hands on the table and leaned so close she could smell the fruity scent of banana on his breath.

"Just tell me where it is. I still don't believe you have one," she said.

"I've already told you, but I see you're not convinced."

"You could...you could take an oath to tell the truth."

"Scouts' honor, hope to die if I tell a lie, swear on—"

"Oh, stop!"

"I haven't even begun."

He moved closer and buried the fingers of one hand in her damp hair. At the same time, he tilted her chin and covered her mouth with his.

Maybe she swooned. She certainly didn't remember standing up, didn't know how she got into his arms. His lips were warm and demanding; he put his whole body into his kisses.

"You're so smooth, so soft." He ran his hands over the bare skin of her back under the sweatshirt.

"This is where . . ." she tried to say.

He kissed her with an open mouth.

"This is where I'm supposed to ask what kind of woman you think I am."

"Sexy, exciting, entertaining . . ."

He was in her ticklish zone, the ribs under her armpits.

She giggled. "Entertaining! Do you expect a song and dance?"

"I expect hurricanes, volcanic eruptions, tidal waves!"

"Those are all disasters!"

His fingers were working magic on her senses. Pretty soon he was going to zero in on two of her more obvious erogenous zones, and she was going to melt like butter in a hot pan.

"I meant you're like natural phenomena—devastating, mind-boggling—"

"With catastrophic consequences!"

"I'll take my chances." He held her so close she had to circle his body with her arms for balance.

His skin felt so good! She rubbed his shoulders, massaged his spine, splayed her fingers over the small of his back. She forgot what they were talking about.

"We shouldn't be doing this," she protested with the forcefulness of a feather duster.

"It's kismet," Joe murmured.

He touched her breasts, fondling them more effectively than she'd dreamed was possible.

"Oh, don't!" Her tone meant *don't stop*.

He caressed her nipples, rolling them between his thumbs and fingers, making them swell and harden until they ached.

"Don't do this?" He bent his head and did something wonderful to her earlobe.

She didn't want him to stop, and then he was kissing her again, making a love feast of her tongue and lips.

He tasted wonderful, and the harder he kissed her, the more impassioned her response became. The skin around her lips tingled hungrily for more. Why had they wasted so much time? They could have been doing this for weeks—years.

Suddenly the world went black. She couldn't see or breathe. Joe had the sweatshirt over her face, and her arms were caught.

"Sorry. This shirt is so big on you."

When she could see again, her breasts were snuggled against his naked torso, bare and free, deliciously tickled by the dark, silky hair on his chest.

What was that warning she'd wanted to give her readers? Watch out for power kisses. Don't be swept away by super...

"I have nicer rooms than the kitchen."

He kissed her throat, trailed his lips to her other earlobe. It made her crazy to be kissed in the hollow below her ear. She needed to surface for air, give this more time.

"If we don't stop now, our column will be X-rated," she said.

"Can't you concentrate on anything but work?" He slid his hands under the loose elastic of the sweats and kneaded her bottom.

"You're squeezing too hard," she gasped.

"I'm torturing myself while you think about your job! Is that all I am to you—column fodder?"

She wasn't ready for that question. It meant admitting things she hadn't analyzed yet—like the way her heart beat faster whenever Joe walked into a room or her hormones kicked in when he lowered his voice in that sexy way he had.

"If I'm more to you than a work buddy, why did you introduce me to Dana DeJong as your co-worker?"

"Because that's how you prefer it." He loosened his hold and stepped back, but she was so agitated she wanted to sock him—or something. "You set boundaries on our relationship from the start," he said. "I don't understand your rule about not dating men you work with."

"I could possibly..." She couldn't bring herself to say it. Instead, she crossed her arms across her breasts, suddenly self-conscious about being naked to the waist.

"Change your mind?" He asked it so quietly his voice soothed her like soft music.

"It's a woman's prerogative," she said meekly.

"You definitely are a woman." He took her in his arms and kissed her with single-minded intensity. "I'm in big trouble," he whispered, covering her face with blissful minikisses and parting her bulkily clad legs with his knee.

"I was thinking the same thing about me."

"I didn't plan this."

"The day hasn't gone quite the way I expected, either."

"About going upstairs..."

"Yes." She really meant, *Yes!*

"I have to go to the store first."

"A store?"

"Drugstore, pharmacy, service station rest room—somewhere!"

"Oh, that kind of store."

"That kind."

"You haven't been practicing safe sex lately?"

"I haven't been practicing any sex at all. The trouble is..." He looked genuinely uncomfortable.

"What?" Was he too shy to buy them? Did he need money? "What, what?"

"I'm scared you won't be here when I get back."

"Oh, is that all?"

"Well, will you?"

"If it doesn't take you more than three or four hours."

"You'll wait that long for me?"

"Will I have to?"

"No way!"

He gave her a vigorous kiss and raced upstairs to put on shoes and a shirt.

He left before she remembered the oversize sweatshirt. She noticed he was wearing a long, loose shirt. She slipped the top back on.

She watched out the window, paced the living room and worked up enough courage to go upstairs to his bedroom.

His furniture matched the rest of the house—a four-piece golden oak set with a queen-size bed. The quilted bed covering was a vintage Southwest design in ocher, desert yellow and midnight blue colors. She peeled back a corner to reveal crisp ivory pillowcases and sheets. She was so nervous that had they been black satin, she might have been sent running.

If she were a real femme fatale, she'd get naked and arrange herself in some eye-catching way on the bed. If she were more sure of herself, she'd lose the baggy sweats and meet him at the top of the stairs when he came back. Instead, she borrowed the brush on his dresser and gave her hair a hundred licks or so, trying to tame it into some semblance of her usual bob.

"Using my brush without asking, I see."

He came up behind her so quietly she shrieked. "Don't scare me like that!"

"Sorry, I thought you were expecting me."

He was holding the little white pharmacy bag so carefully she was reminded of a TV commercial that used a plastic bag full of live bees.

"I guess so—I mean I was."

He kicked off the thongs he'd worn to drive to the store. When he yanked the shirt over his head, she saw he hadn't forgotten her while he did his errand.

"Would you like to do something else first, maybe eat?" he offered. "There's no rush."

She smiled and tears of tenderness clouded her vision. She blinked them away; this was no time to start sniffling.

"You really are a very nice man."

"Where did that come from?" He stepped closer.

"I have a sentimental side."

"I'd like to know about all your sides," he said.

"Sometimes you're the one who talks too much!"

She untied the cord that was keeping the oversize sweats around her waist. They dropped to a bulky pile around her feet, and she stepped free of them—right into his arms.

"You're beautiful," he whispered, kissing her closed lids, the tip of her nose, her cheeks and chin.

He had strong lips. They could make her mouth do anything he wanted: pucker, stretch, open, close.

"You taste delicious," he murmured.

She felt like a medical-book drawing of the nervous system, and her whole network lit up like a Christmas tree. She could feel every kiss from the top of her head to the soles of her feet.

"Amy." He didn't stop kissing her. "Let me—" he found the pulse point in her throat and gave it special attention "—take this shirt off."

"I'll be naked." Who was this idiot speaking with her voice?

"That's the idea." Not satisfied with kissing her ear, he explored it with the tip of his tongue, making her squeal in approval.

"Only if you're naked, too." Ah, she could trust this voice emanating from a part of her brain she'd forgotten about.

"Sounds fair." He was already freeing her arms.

She gave an involuntary shiver, but not because the room was too cool. She felt warm enough to heat up the inside of a refrigerator.

"Now do me," he challenged sweetly, bringing her hands to his waist.

"Oh, my." Easier said than done.

She slid her fingers below his tan line, loving the smooth, cool texture of the skin on his back. Then, delight of delights, she slipped her hands under the elastic in back and felt his bottom tighten under her touch. She kneaded until he relaxed, then toyed with him until he moaned.

"What are you trying to do to me?" he asked.

"Make you crazy."

"I'm already crazy for you. Take my shorts off."

"They're stuck."

"You're a problem solver."

"It's a hard one."

"You're telling me!"

She did what had to be done, telling herself it was only a muscle. But ordinary muscles didn't protrude from a nest of silky dark hair or have a sheath of smooth skin. His shorts slid to the floor, and there was nothing between them.

"Let me feel you," he said.

She swayed in his arms, transported by his lips on her shoulders and breasts, his hand between her thighs.

"Wait a second," he said.

It would take an earthquake to move her.

He did what he had to do, then stripped the bed cover off the bed. The venetian blinds were closed; she couldn't remember when that had happened. The dusky light was enough to see his long, lean, breathtakingly muscular frame and the wide expanse of sheeted mattress.

His pause had given her time to think of consequences, but not the will to do anything to prevent them.

He lifted her off the floor, sweeping her into his arms and surprising her into delighted compliance. She grasped his shoulders, pleasantly stunned by his masterly gesture.

Slowly he lowered her to the middle of the bed, laying her down with her head cushioned by a pillow, and looking down on her with an expression that went light-years beyond his mushy look.

"I want this to be the best ever for both of us," he said softly.

It already was for her.

He made love to her shoulders and breasts, but when she grew languid, content to bask in his tender ministrations, he raised her to new heights of active and excited participation.

Several times she thought the moment had come, but each time he managed to prolong it, to heighten her anticipation. He kissed the tips of her fingers, the tops of her toes, the dimpled hollow at the small of her back. She explored the neat little hollow of his navel, the tiny knobs of his nipples, even the bony hardness of his knees. She found muscles as unyielding as steel bands and soft, vulnerable spots where he was as ticklish as she was.

She instinctively recognized the moment when holding back became agony for him. There was no awkward fumbling, no painful probing, no false starts. They came together like two halves of a whole. She'd never been ready like this, never felt such wild pulsations. Her secret spot responded to his earthshaking shudders, and magic happened.

Wow! She didn't know whether she said it out loud or not.

"You're fantastic." He collapsed on top of her, the weight of his legs between hers, his elbows saving her from feeling crushed.

"Oh, Joe!" That said it all.

He tenderly kissed her closed lids, swollen lips, sensitive breasts. "Thank-you kisses," he murmured, rolling beside her and pressing her wrist against his lips.

"That was..." What could she say that was adequate? He'd elevated her, made her feel special—desirable. Made being a woman seem a high calling.

"You're wonderful, Joe." She'd never been more sincere.

"Come here."

She didn't need urging. They cuddled and slept.

Joe woke up first, his arm and shoulders stiff from holding Amy against him as they napped. In spite of this minor discomfort, he'd never had such an overwhelming sense of well-being. Every cell in his body felt renewed, refreshed. If this was euphoria, he could understand why mystics, fanatics and addicts followed bizarre and sometimes self-destructive paths to achieve it.

Sex had never done this for him before—before Amy. She seemed smaller and more vulnerable with her head cradled in the crook of his arm, her hair in disarray and tickling him. He loved that startling shade of copper, the feathery lashes that looked longer when her eyes were shut, her graceful hands and slender fingers.

He'd been right about her body. She was more beautiful naked than clothed. She seemed to be molded as a whole, not assembled from diverse parts. Her breasts filled his hands without feeling heavy; the pinkish brown tips were endearingly youthful but so womanly he felt new stirrings just thinking of them in the unlit room. Her legs— he was crazy about her legs. And her bottom was so cute and round he wanted to wake her up with a love pat.

He was ready again, but he was kidding himself, too. It wasn't her luscious body that made Amy Patterson special. They could spend a month in bed together and he'd still want more from her. He just didn't know what.

She couldn't be owned; the thought of taming her was ludicrous. They could clash over something as trivial as the use of a prepositional phrase, and she was so damned ambitious he'd like to shut down her computer terminal permanently.

He tried to imagine Amy waiting for him after work with a home-cooked meal on the table and a smile for her provider and protector. That fantasy didn't work even if all she was wearing was a frilly see-through apron and three-inch heels.

She stirred and sleepily stretched her length against his side.

"I still don't know," she mumbled.

"Don't know what?" Her wiggling was arousing him again.

"Whether you have a tattoo."

He laughed, rolling onto his side away from her and clutching his knees in the fetal position.

"Well, do you?"

"The light switch is by the door if you really want to know." He stayed curled on his side.

"I do." She bounced the mattress in her eagerness to satisfy her curiosity.

The overhead fixture glowed too brightly for comfort.

"It has to be someplace that was covered by those gray shorts."

"You checked pretty carefully, did you?" He was having a hard time holding back his laughter.

"Let me see."

She knelt on the bed and gave his backside a hands-on examination.

"I think you made it up," she accused him.

He rolled over onto his back and lay there spread-eagled for her inspection, then hastily covered his new erection with a corner of the top sheet. After all they'd done, he couldn't believe how embarrassed he felt.

"You do!"

She touched it.

"Joe Malone, that is obscene!"

"I admit to being dumb and drunk when I got it."

"But why there?"

"I didn't want to take my briefs off for a lady tattoo artist."

"Phoenix rising on your inner thigh! Didn't it hurt?" She touched the colorful mythical bird.

"Like a burning needle from hell! I haven't been out-of-control drunk since then."

She started to giggle, then laughed uproariously. Her breasts bounced, and he wanted her even more than he had the first time, impossible as that seemed.

"I'm ready again," she said, tumbling on top of him, her cheeks rosy from mirth.

She reached over to the nightstand and took responsibility from him, then slid onto him easily, as if they'd been partners for years.

Something had been troubling him, but he forgot everything with her torso swaying over him and the rising tide of rapture engulfing both of them.

They ate peanut butter and jelly sandwiches at 3:00 a.m. and read the Sunday *Monitor* in bed together at noon. She was shy in the shower at first, and as slippery as the greased pole his frat had made him climb when he was a pledge, but once they got the knack, there was no limit to what they could accomplish together.

At last, driven out by hunger, he raced to a Chinese restaurant and came back with enough wire-handled cardboard containers to provide leftovers for a week.

After one for the road at dusk on Sunday, she insisted on going home.

"I thought I'd just keep you," he teased, wondering why she didn't look as beat as he felt.

"As your love slave?"

She was straddling him, her bare bottom on his stomach, but all he could feel at this point was amusement.

"Whatever works for you." He pulled her down and softly kissed her overused lips. "With you, everything seems to work," he whispered, stroking her thighs with the vague hope of keeping her there.

"We have to go to work in the morning," she reminded him.

He groaned in protest and pulled a pillow over his face.

"Come on, Malone." She crawled off the bed and pulled open dresser drawers until she found his supply of sweats.

"Next time you come, bring your own clothes."

He didn't care what she borrowed; he wanted reassurance that there would be a next time.

"Think how it cuts down on my laundry if I wear your stuff."

Her bare back looked too delicate for the old green sweats she was tying at her waist. He wanted to take care of her, cherish her.

"Get your butt out of bed," she demanded.

He also wanted to strangle her when she played the tough-girl reporter he remembered from high school.

"I'm yours to command," he said, reluctantly getting up to drive her home.

9

Amy had a glow. Joe knew that women looked that way after sex, but he'd never seen radiance last so long. He couldn't pinpoint any physical difference, but she was more beautiful than ever.

They'd spent the morning trying to pretend nothing had happened over the weekend. He envied the way she tapped away on the keyboard, filling her screen with volumes of words while his concentration was nil. His only consolation was that she repeatedly muttered to herself and deleted whole passages.

"Let's take the rest of the day off," he suggested when it was time for lunch. He had in mind a nooner that would last until midnight.

"Sorry, I don't even have time to go out for lunch. I don't know how I got so far behind."

"You seem to be catching up." He tried not to sound disappointed.

"I roughed out my half of next Sunday's installment. Do you want to take a look at it?"

"No, I think our original system is better—work independently so we don't influence each other's answers."

"Does that mean I can't read what you're writing for Sunday?"

"We made a deal. You can see it when I get it done."

"No, if you're willing to let me read it, I don't need to. If you're going to lunch, would you mind bringing me back a tuna sandwich? The vending machine's all out."

"You should walk over with me. Too much sitting will make your rear end spread," he said, trying to tease her into going.

"Thank you for your sage advice," she said coolly.

"Sweetheart, I just said that because I want you to come with me. You have a fantastic behind."

"Joe, that isn't something you say to a co-worker." She glanced toward the door as though she expected the whole newsroom to be standing there listening.

"You do if you've just spent twenty-four hours playing mattress games."

"Listen to you! Playing games!"

"Would you like it better if I said twenty-four hours of bliss, of better sex than I'd ever imagined?"

"I knew this would happen!" She stood and confronted him with arms folded over her chest. "Men can never separate business and pleasure. Just because we're friendly outside the office doesn't mean you should treat me like your little plaything at work."

"Did I kiss you good morning? Fondle your breast? Cop a feel?" He was making the situation worse, but he was too annoyed to stop. "I know what sexual harassment is, but you've given me plenty of reasons to believe my attentions aren't unwelcome."

"Give me some credit! I wasn't thinking of suing you, but you're proving everything I've said about office relationships is true. If we're going to be partners at work and friends—"

"Lovers."

"Friends outside of work, we need some rules."

"Lady, you know what you can do with your rules."

He stalked out, but it didn't give him much satisfaction.

* * *

Amy wanted to cry, but she wouldn't give him the satisfaction of seeing her with puffy eyes and a red nose. All she'd wanted to do was keep her personal life separate from her work. He didn't come back with her tuna sandwich, and she couldn't have swallowed it if he had.

In fact, he didn't return to work at all that day, but she didn't let it interfere with her job. By the time she went home that evening, the sun was low in the sky and her wrists ached from too many hours at the computer without a break.

"Ring, damn you," she said to her phone when she got home. There was no message from Joe on the answering machine, and he didn't call that evening.

She wanted to phone in sick the next morning, but she had to face him again sometime. The longer she delayed, the harder it would be.

Did she owe him an apology? Did he owe her one? Did it matter whether they kept score of the little hurts they inflicted on each other?

He didn't come to the office on Tuesday morning, either, and there was no message to explain his absence.

When he did show up after 2:00 p.m., he brought a disk and transferred work to the office computer.

"You worked at home this morning."

"Yes."

"Get much done?" She was making an effort to sound normal. If he wanted to sulk, let him.

"Some. I don't have your single-minded devotion to duty."

"What you have is a lousy attitude."

They were civil the rest of the week, but Amy cried three times in the women's rest room because he treated her like a piece of office furniture. If he noticed her blotchy complexion and red eyes, he didn't mention it.

Ed called Saturday afternoon, and she agreed to go with him to a concert at the university; she didn't want to be home alone moping over Joe. Ed picked her up that evening, and she fought sleep for hours while a string quartet played an endless selection of new pieces, most of them composed with deep, slow-moving rivers in mind.

When Ed gave her a big, wet kiss and a hopeful leer at her door, she dumped him—this time for good. She preferred being miserable alone to being bored and miserable with him.

She was up, dressed and still in a terrible mood at nine the next morning, too depressed to make plans for the day. When the doorbell rang, she raced to open the door, her heart pounding in her throat.

Joe was standing there, his dark mahogany hair rumpled over the angriest deep blue eyes she'd ever seen.

"You used me!" He thrust a single folded sheet of newsprint under her nose, making her back up enough for him to come inside and slam the door.

"I guess this means no breakfast in bed." Her lame joke got the reaction it deserved—none.

"I thought we were writing about the wedding. You wrote a tirade warning women not to be taken in by sex."

"I wasn't writing about you!"

"Listen to this." He scanned her piece, picking out scattered phrases. "'A looong time between kisses'—try using your spellcheck—'a burning desire to get physical,' 'mistake lust for love,' 'taken in by a handsome face,' 'give in to urges,' 'don't mistake it for the real thing...'"

"You're taking it out of context!"

"I'm taking it damn poorly!"

"Let me see what you wrote." She snatched the column from him and read rapidly, knowing almost immediately she didn't have a case against him. He'd written a gentle, good-humored piece about recognizing a relationship that was going someplace.

"It's nice." What else could she say?

"I know you have a lot of quirks, Patterson, but I didn't think male-bashing was one of them."

"This isn't male-bashing. I love men!" One especially. "I just thought it was my job—"

"'Just' think about this. I'm tired of being column fodder."

"You went out with me only because Garver made it part of an assignment."

"Believe that if you like. You were right about one thing. Trying to have a personal relationship with a co-worker is a good way to invite disaster."

"Now you say that—after you got me in bed. Now it's convenient to agree with me so you can wiggle out of making a comm—"

"If I wanted to avoid commitment, I wouldn't use your harebrained theories as an excuse."

"You can't talk to me that way!"

"I am. Don't try to hang a seduction rap on me. You were just as eager—"

"It's not my fault you're the sexiest man I've ever met!"

Now she had blown it! She might as well admit she'd had a thing for him when she was sixteen, and the impact of seeing him again had nearly knocked her off her feet. No, she couldn't give him that much satisfaction!

"So you used me for the column and for kicks?"

"You are the most egotistical, self-centered, conceited man—"

"Also the sexiest." His face was grim, and his voice was harsh.

"Was I on target in this or what?" She crumpled the page with the column and threw it at him. "Women need to be warned about sexy devils who prey on them!"

"Next you'll accuse me of trying to con you out of your life savings."

"I don't have any—and I never intended the column to be about you. If you take it personally, it just proves business and personal relationships don't mesh."

"You've convinced me," he said stiffly. "No more mixing business with pleasure."

He left.

She'd made her point, but she wasn't a winner. Her tear ducts overflowed.

She spent most of the afternoon trying to get rid of the headache she'd gotten from crying.

All her Monday-morning omens were bad. She broke a fingernail, dribbled coffee from the wet grounds on her skirt and got an early call from her mother. The Silver Fox was taking her to Monte Carlo for a week; they were starting to make long-term plans together. Would Amy water her plants?

The thought of acquiring a stepfather with a gold tooth was depressing enough, but she had to go to the office and face Joe.

He was sitting at his terminal when she got there.

"I thought maybe you were going to call in sick again," he said.

"I have too much to do."

"Start with the mail."

"I can plan my own work schedule, thank you."

"Okay, don't start with the mail. But you might be interested in the piece on top."

She picked up a letter still in the opened envelope, mad at herself because she was so predictable when it came to her curiosity.

"This is from our publisher, William III."

"Obviously."

She quickly scanned the short note. "He really does like the column! Garver wasn't just manipulating us by using his name."

"More importantly, he thinks it's boosting circulation."

"That's—" she remembered the tension between them in time to contain her excitement "—very nice."

"I've set aside some letters I think might work for the column. If you don't like them, we won't use them. Other than that, the only thing we have to do together is decide on a topic we both can live with for next Sunday's column."

She must have been crazy to think she was falling in love with this... this domineering male.

"I haven't given it any thought yet," she lied.

"Let me know when you have."

He sauntered away, hands stuffed in the deep pockets of his dove gray pleated trousers.

She didn't see him again that day.

That evening, she made a futile attempt to dissuade her mother from letting a strange man take her abroad. Failing as expected, she agreed to be diligent in her duties during her week of plant patrol. What else did she have to do with her evenings?

She had no one but herself to blame for the sad state of her own love life. It was inevitable, as soon as her relationship with Joe became personal, that they would have problems at work. Now she had to face him in the office, remembering all the intimate details of their wild weekend. She was sure he would never think of her as a competent professional equal again.

She was tempted to quit. The *Monitor* didn't need two advice columnists. She could always get a job doing something else, like...

Or she could move, live somewhere else—Denver, Kalamazoo, the Aleutians.

Tuesday she worked alone in the morning, went out for lunch with Roberta and came back to find a suggestion from Joe on her e-mail. It was a peculiar way to communicate, considering he was sitting within spitting distance of her desk.

"A double date is a good idea," she said to him after she read it. Funny how she missed him the most when he was in the same room with her.

"If you have any trouble getting a date—" he began.

"I understand—we'll be going with different people. I can handle my part of the assignment."

"It will give us a different slant for the next installment."

"I said I understand, Joe. Where, when and what time?"

"Tomorrow, if that's not too soon."

He probably thought she couldn't get a date on such short notice "Fine."

Could she undump Ed for just one evening? Maybe, if she told him the *Monitor* was buying dinner.

"Meet here in the parking lot, seven o'clock," Joe ordered.

"Seven-thirty would be better," she said, determined to have some control. "We'll go in separate cars."

"All right. I'll make dinner reservations to be sure we have them."

"How kind of you to bring up our last snafu."

"Knock it off, Amy."

"I don't want to do anything to irritate you."

It was the only bright spot in her day—at least he cared enough to be annoyed.

She dutifully overwatered her mother's plants on the way home, even though her globe-trotting parent had been gone only a few hours. It would save her from running over after work tomorrow—she was counting the restaurant rendezvous with Joe and his date as hard labor.

After delaying the unpleasant task of trying to get a date as long as she dared, she dialed Ed's number, heard him answer and hung up without saying anything. She wouldn't grovel just so she could show up with a man who thought it was clever to make a waitress stand by the table for a half hour while he quizzed her on the menu entrées.

She remembered her canceled blind date and decided a double dose of misery would at least put her back in her matchmaking friend's good graces.

Dale—his name was Dale VanderPlant—checked his social calendar and decided he could squeeze in a free dinner.

She picked out her outfit ahead of time so she wouldn't have to debate with herself when she rushed home to change. The funeral black suit would do fine. Just to show Joe he was missing something, she decided to wear a new décolletage-style bra she'd been too chicken to wear before and a yellow silk tank top that would give her old suit a sporty look.

After this date, she was going to insist on winging the rest of the installments on dating etiquette in the nineties. She'd had it with pretend dates, arranged dates and blind dates. Dale didn't know it, but he was getting dumped right after dessert.

Joe got to the *Monitor* parking lot on time and in no mood to wait for Amy and her date. He'd already exhausted his store of small talk during the drive there, but Belinda didn't seem bothered by his inattentiveness. She talked nonstop with only an occasional word from him to indicate he was still awake.

He shouldn't have been so quick to throw away the phone numbers he got at Hair Amore and Tommy O'Malley's. Coming up with a date on such short notice hadn't been easy after being gone so long. He had to assume most of his former girlfriends were married or otherwise unavailable. Much as he hated admitting the wisdom of it, he'd followed Amy's rule about not dating co-workers. He didn't want someone at the *Monitor* to have a grudge against him when he didn't ask for a second date.

He'd had a stroke of luck—maybe good, maybe bad—when he'd parked his car last night. Belinda had been walking her silly-looking poodle, the poor dog weighed down by rhinestones and bows, and he'd said hello to this neighbor enough times in the past to make striking up a conversation easy. She'd looked pretty cute in shorts and halter with her streaky blond hair pulled back in a ponytail. Unfortunately, she dressed herself for their date with the same fashion know-how she used with her pet. Her dress, what there was of it, was covered with orange sequins, and she was wearing enough rhinestone jewelry to weigh down the victim of a mob hit better than concrete overshoes.

Worse, her shoes were nothing but big silver bows with clear plastic heels, and she had enough makeup on her face for a circus act. Patterson was going to have a field day writing about this double date! He wanted to kick himself for giving her the opportunity.

"Is that them?" Belinda pointed at a big gray Buick not unlike the one his grandfather had used to tool around Texas since his retirement.

He got out and walked to the passenger window Amy had rolled down.

"Joe, this is Dale."

First names. Good. He couldn't remember Belinda's last name.

"Nice to meet you," he said. The other guy nodded.

Joe didn't try to reach through the window across Amy to shake hands. Her date had baby-fine blond hair with a fifty-dollar haircut to make it look casual. His molded-to-the-shoulders stockbroker blue suit made Joe feel like a slob in jeans and his old olive sport jacket. Without seeing the guy's feet, he was willing to bet he was wearing Italian loafers with tassels.

"We have reservations at Roxy's. I hope they hold them," he said, to point out they'd kept him waiting.

"Oh, are we late?" Amy asked.

Her feigned innocence didn't work with him—not anymore.

The restaurant was trendy enough to make Belinda twitter and old Dale click the heels of his shiny gray loafers—no tassels but an insert of woven material on the tops. Amy looked as if she was sucking on a lemon. He sincerely hoped Dale was a total pain in the butt.

At least the decor didn't grate on his nerves. It was low-key Southwestern pastels with dim lighting and no fake cacti or bogus Anasazi pottery to make it look like a tourist trap. The light jazz piped over speakers was a pleasant change from typical restaurant background music. It made him mellow enough to go with the flow and order a margarita when the others did.

The evening took a turn for the worse when their tuxedoed waiter set a blue drink in front of him.

"Oh, isn't it pretty," Belinda cooed.

Amy looked as if she'd rather drink rattlesnake venom.

"My favorite color," Dale said, making a big deal out of toasting "new friends."

Joe felt like an idiot clicking the huge goblets.

The menu offered a combination of Santa-Fe style dishes and nouvelle cuisine. He did take grim satisfaction in imagining Bug's face when he saw a dinner for four at these prices on his expense account. "Order whatever you'd like," he said.

Joe decided on lamb chops with prickly-pear fritters and sweet potatoes with green chilies. He didn't pay any attention to what the others ordered, but he wished Amy would button her jacket, preferably up to her neck. Her breasts were pushed up and out under a low-cut yellow top that made them more conspicuous than a stripper's pasties.

Dale was ogling her chest and trying to impress Belinda with his financial wizardry at the same time.

"I have no idea what an investment consultant does," Belinda said.

"He consults on investments," Dale said, laughing at his own wit or lack thereof.

The man couldn't seem to say two consecutive sentences without punctuating them with tag lines—okeydokey, you betcha, gotcha, yes sirreee. Joe was only slightly less interested in the guy's racketball scores and sweater collection than in his stock portfolio.

"My grandmother left me a small inheritance, really so teeny-weeny it's hardly worth mentioning, but I wonder if there's some way I could invest it," Belinda cooed.

Dale had enough suggestions to dominate the conversation until the after-dinner ice-cream drinks came. Amy abstained; Joe had a Scotch on the rocks. For some strange reason, his tattoo was itching. He stoically resisted scratching it.

"Tomorrow is a workday," Amy said.

Joe looked directly at her face, but she wouldn't make eye contact.

"You know, I really would like another cuppa," Dale said, flagging down a passing waiter.

"Excuse me," Amy said. "I'm going to the powder room. Would you like to come?"

She looked at Belinda but didn't say her name. It was the first time that evening Amy had spoken directly to her, and Joe amused himself for a moment wondering if she was harboring a little green monster.

Unlikely, he decided, polishing off his Scotch with a gloomy thought. Amy probably thought he deserved Belinda.

Belinda declined, and Amy left the dining area alone. He couldn't help watching the womanly sway of her hips, subtle but seductive. She was wearing little black pumps, and he wanted to tell her how her walk turned him on.

Dummy! The last thing she wanted to hear was a compliment from him.

He couldn't stand his itchy tattoo another minute. Maybe he should have the damn thing surgically removed. Amy had gotten a kick out of it, but he couldn't imagine showing it to another woman. He excused himself and went in search of the men's room.

Joe returned to the table, hoping he could pick up the bill and get out of there. He had enough bad things to say about double dates to do a whole new series.

The check was there in a black leather folder, but the table was deserted.

Amy came up behind him. "Where are they?"

"Rest rooms?"

"Belinda's not in there, and I didn't pass her on the way."

"Ah, the old message-on-the-dinner-chit trick," he said, reading more than the meal charge on the bill. "They've split. Together."

"Really?"

"Dale has to do some urgent investment consulting."

"What a break!"

"I did the best I could on short notice," he admitted glumly.

"A friend insisted I meet Dale."

"Well, you've met him."

"I think they're perfect together."

"They deserve each other anyway. Let's go."

"I'll have to call a cab. I rode here with the financial wizard." She opened her purse and started sorting coins.

"Don't be silly. I'll give you a ride."

"It's out of your way. I'll manage."

"We're working tonight, aren't we? I'll put in for the mileage. Let me sign for the bill, and we'll go."

"I'm overwhelmed by your generous offer."

Driving her home, he tried to come up with bland observations and meaningless comments, but her response was nil.

He still wanted to tell her to button her jacket.

When they arrived at her brightly lit apartment complex, he stopped as close to her entrance as he could, blocking other cars so he could watch her go inside. He didn't offer to walk upstairs with her. He was mad, but he wasn't made of stone.

10

Amy had to check her date book at the office to be sure it was Friday. Only one thing made this day different from all the other depressing days that week—Joe was working in the office instead of avoiding her by writing at home.

He made a short day of it. At three o'clock he was ready to leave.

"Are you still going to the spring dance?" he asked.

Was she? She'd been trying to forget the invitation from their old high school.

"You probably should," he went on, not giving her time to come up with a no-show excuse. "We're the guests of honor, the old grads who made good, the couple they're counting on to start the ball rolling."

"I get the picture. I'll see you there."

"I could swing by for you."

He couldn't sound less enthusiastic if he'd just offered to take out her garbage.

"I'd rather take my own car."

And that's how I ended up going to the ball by myself like Cinderella in her pumpkin coach, Amy thought as she watched him make tracks through the newsroom.

Darned if she'd make a big deal out of a dance for kids by buying a new dress or having her hair done. Her navy dress and her everyday bob would have to do, and if she looked like one of the chaperons, it didn't matter.

* * *

Saturday night, standing alone in front of the flower-bedecked trellis that transformed the door to the school gym into a teenage version of a romantic fantasy, Amy fervently wished she hadn't sloughed Joe off. The passing years hadn't changed one thing—she still felt like a wallflower.

"Amy Patterson! It's great to see you! Will you let an old teacher be the first to reserve a dance?"

"Mr. Phelps, hello."

She'd had a mad crush on this English teacher her senior year. In spite of some silver in his once jet black hair, he still looked like a French movie star.

"None of that 'Mr. Phelps' stuff. Call me Russ. Come on, Amy, I'll introduce you to some of the chaperons, as we laughingly call ourselves."

The junior class had outdone themselves in decorating for the dance. Tinsel stars hung from the ceiling, and huge sparkly cardboard cutouts of dancing couples lined the walls, almost obscuring the concrete-block construction and the folded bleachers.

Joe, looking somber in his dark suit, was already chatting with Coach Baker. She nodded at him and let Mr. Phelps—how could she possibly call one of her old teachers Russ?—sweep her along the line of parents and faculty members drafted for dance duty. Mr. Higgins, the physics teacher who'd terrified her and ruined her average with a *C,* pressed her hand with his soft, damp palm and actually leered at her.

How odd to be seeing teachers as people. She rather enjoyed it.

"Just before the band starts playing, I'll introduce you and Joe, then the two of you can start the festivities by dancing the first dance together," the English teacher said.

She glanced at Joe and hoped she wouldn't have to ask him to dance with her.

She didn't. With a dutiful smile, he came to claim her as a dance partner and took her arm, probably so she wouldn't embarrass him by falling on the newly waxed floor.

"Smile," he ordered curtly. "Pretend you want to dance with me."

She didn't notice the music; she was totally oblivious to everyone and everything in the room except Joe. He was holding her in his arms, but it didn't mean anything to him. She held back tears with difficulty.

Afterward he thanked her for the dance.

She'd planned an early escape—like Cinderella dashing away so fast she loses her glass slipper. She hadn't counted on being the belle of the ball.

Mr. Phelps revealed that he was divorced. During their first dance, he told Amy the reasons his wife of thirteen years had left him. By the time the band went out for intermission, she'd actually managed to call him Russ once.

Not that the English teacher was her only partner; she could hardly keep track of all the men who swept her across the floor. She went from the arms of the football captain to the dry-handed grasp of Mr. Depopolus, who'd retired from the faculty when she was twelve years old. Men even cut in, a novel experience that prompted her to look longingly in Joe's direction several times. He was spending most of his time on the sidelines. Every time she caught his eye, he was nursing a cup of sugary red punch or gabbing with one of his old teachers.

She envied him. He got to sit, and he wasn't being stalked by an oversexed faculty member. Mr. Phelps waylaid her every chance he got, none too subtly declaring his eligibility and his youthful point of view.

She'd never suspected that being popular was so exhausting. Her face ached from smiling, and her feet felt as if she'd been running barefoot on cobblestones. Mr. Phelps told her he was eager to have more children while he was still virile. She wondered if one of the kids had spiked the punch.

Once, she nearly made her escape from the dance via the rest room, but dear old Mr. Fitzsimmons, the teacher who'd gently guided her through the mysteries of geometry, begged for a dance. After that, the football team seemed to be having a contest to see who could dance with the billboard babe the most times. Mr. Phelps looked frustrated.

Joe didn't ask for a second dance.

She didn't get a chance to leave until the band was packing their instruments. By then, Mr. Phelps had made it clear he wanted her to have his babies. She didn't see Joe anywhere along her escape route.

Go figure, she thought as she drove away. Now that only one man in the world mattered to her, she'd had them falling at her feet. She felt as if she'd been at a tractor pull—suspended between two monsters going in opposite directions.

She was too hyper to sleep, too keyed up to go home. She didn't have the stomach to go to a bar; Mr. Phelps was all the would-be stud she could handle in one evening. She couldn't think of anyone, however dear a friend by daylight, who would be thrilled to have her visit at that hour.

Rather than go home, she headed for Sun City. Her mother wouldn't be there, but she could water the damn plants and save doing it tomorrow.

The condo environs were quiet, with most of the residents tucked in for the night, but an outdoor light made it easy to find the keyhole in her mother's door and gain entry. Once inside, she turned on lights in every room to chase away the gloom and filled a long-spouted watering can.

She made quick work of the spider plants in the kitchen, thirsty little devils that they were. Every parent plant had dozens of offspring on slender, ropey vines, and it was testimony to her mother's busy social life that she hadn't potted a hundred or so to give to her closest friends.

The hanging ferns in the living room required more care; she didn't want her mother to come home to a jungle of droopy yellow botanical casualties. Then she opened the sliding glass door and went out to water the array of plants on the patio. She made herself pay attention so she wouldn't water a cactus by mistake. It took awhile, but the pot of mums was the last . . .

Mums! Her mother didn't raise mums. The fluffy yellow flowers had come from a florist. They still had crackly green foil and a big white bow around the pot.

She looked more carefully, wondering why she hadn't noticed it on her last trip. Probably she'd been too preoccupied with her problems.

"So, my little hothouse beauties, what are you doing in my mother's jungle?"

A small white envelope was stuck on a plastic stick and nearly lost among the blooms. She shouldn't read it. She actually walked away, but curiosity overcame her scruples. Anyway, her mother wouldn't have left the card in the pot if she wanted to keep the donor's identity a secret.

She carefully removed the envelope and pulled out a rectangular card embellished with a tiny Cupid.

Darling, you've made my life worth living again.

There was no signature.

Tears of guilt welled up in her eyes as she imagined what it must mean to two people who'd lost beloved partners to find each other. She'd been so selfish, resenting the Silver Fox—she had to start thinking of him by name when she remembered it—because he was taking her father's place. This wasn't about her, and it had nothing to do with her father. It was about loneliness and loving, and who was she to pass judgment?

And why was she letting love slip through her fingers? Was her job really so important? Why had she quarreled with Joe? When had she become so rigid and demanding that she was willing to sacrifice happiness for principles that hardly mattered at all in the grand scheme of life?

She had a good cry—good because it washed away a lot of bad stuff and left her mind clear and unclouded by life's nonessentials.

She loved Joe Malone.

Everything else was irrelevant.

She cried some more. She didn't have a clue what to do about loving him. Joe was barely civil, and she didn't know how to win his love.

Monday morning she went to work with new resolve.

No matter what Joe said or did, she wasn't going to give up without the fight of her life.

He came in late, hands stuffed in the pockets of pale gray pleated slacks. He was wearing a deep blue broadcloth shirt, the top three buttons open to reveal a sprinkling of dark hair on golden skin. She had to look away so he wouldn't guess how the sight of him made her feel— limp, languid and aroused all at the same time.

"Morning." He mumbled like a man with a mouthful of marbles.

"Good morning."

That's it, be crisp and businesslike, she told herself, buoyed up by the plan she'd struggled to perfect all day Sunday.

"I didn't see you leave the dance," he said. "I thought we might have gone out for a drink."

"I left when the band stopped playing."

"Have a good time?"

"Yes, thank you."

"I had that English teacher, Phelps, for senior comp. He was always dropping chalk or his pen, then stooping so he could look up the girls' skirts. I guess he's still a randy old devil."

He wanted to know if she'd left with Russ. She had no intention of confirming or denying it.

"I suppose we could get some column inches out of the dance," he said halfheartedly when she wasn't forthcoming with any information to satisfy his curiosity.

"Possibly."

"Well, let's get to work."

She didn't point out that she was already working—only not for the *Monitor*'s benefit.

When she was satisfied with her special piece, she hurried off and called in some favors. Her new copy would appear in Wednesday's edition of the column. Now there was nothing to do but cross her fingers and make sure she didn't wear any unlucky clothing, like the green panties she'd been wearing when she had her last fender-bender. When she went out for lunch, she was careful not to step on cracks in the sidewalk. She wasn't a total believer, but it couldn't hurt to be a little bit superstitious.

The morning edition was outside her door earlier than usual Wednesday. A good omen. The carrier hadn't overslept as he often did.

Her hands were unsteady as she spread the paper on her kitchen table and turned to the column.

Dear Readers,
It's easier to give advice to other people than to solve a big problem of my own. Can anyone help me with this one?

Why did she do this to herself? Exposing her feelings for Joe in print suddenly seemed more embarrassing than walking through the mall with a streamer of toilet tissue trailing behind her.

"No time to be a sissy," she muttered, forcing herself to read to the end.

> So you see, readers, we had a good thing going, but I blew it. What can I do to get him back?

She hadn't mentioned his name, hadn't revealed intimate details about their wonderful weekend. But Joe would know she meant him.

She still had to do the hardest thing of all—go to work as though she hadn't confessed her love for him in the public press.

He might laugh at her.

He might be infuriated.

She wouldn't blame him if he never spoke to her again. He might even refuse to continue working on the column with her.

Driving to work, she imagined every horrible scenario from Joe publicly rebuking her to giving her the silent treatment and never uttering another word to her for the rest of his life. She was so scared she drove past her exit and wasted twenty minutes backtracking in morning rush-hour traffic. She wouldn't even have the advantage of getting there first and pretending to ignore him when he came in.

"This isn't me," she said, checking her face in the rearview mirror before she left the safety of her car in the parking lot. "My body has been taken over by an alien, something slimy with seven legs and a really bad case of halitosis. People will run for their lives when I walk into the building, and I'll have to face Joe all alone."

She wished—no, she didn't.

It seemed as if she spent a week or two walking at least a hundred miles from the parking lot to her fish-tank office. She stiffened her face with a dopey smile and said, "Good morning," in a remote voice to every moving blur she passed on the way. No one seemed to suspect she was really that other being.

Why hadn't she thought of the consequences of going public? The idea had seemed devastatingly clever at dawn Sunday when she concocted her plan. Maybe lack of sleep had curdled her brain.

Joe was in the office.

She could see his broad shoulders and strong back encased in blue denim, his dark hair curling seductively over the shirt collar.

He was going to kill her!

His screen was on, and he seemed engrossed in something.

He was going to ridicule her until the blood vessels in her cheeks burst from blushing.

She wanted to go home—to Mommy.

He glanced up when she came into their cubicle. "Morning. Get stuck in traffic?"

"Something like that."

"I started the mail. The legal department has a question on the advice we gave that woman going through a divorce—our documentation should satisfy them. And maintenance will be up today to check the squeak in your chair."

"Is that all I missed being twenty minutes late to work?" Her voice sounded squeaky.

"Basically that's it." He turned back to his screen and continued to pound on the keyboard.

He must not have read the column. She put her purse away, horrified to see the morning *Monitor* folded newsboy-style on the corner of his desk.

Joe didn't touch it the whole day. He couldn't have avoided it more scrupulously if the paper had been radioactive.

He's read it, and he's torturing me, she concluded when she got back from lunch to find the paper still in the same position on the desk.

Thursday was even worse. The Wednesday paper was still on his desk. She knew he'd read it. Why was he doing this to her?

A few answers to her column question trickled in that afternoon. It was amazing how fast letters moved across town when she wanted them to come via Siberia.

"I'll sort this mail," she volunteered.

He nodded compliance and asked if her chair was better now that it'd been greased.

A real avalanche of mail arrived Friday. Her fans liked giving advice even better than reading it, and letters came up from the mailroom in record quantities.

"Are you guys running a lottery?" the mail clerk asked, disgruntled by the extra work generated by their column.

"Don't worry about sorting the mail," Amy told Joe. "I'll take care of it."

He watched with a bemused expression while she tried to find a temporary place to pile the stacks of letters.

"Need any help?" he asked.

"No! No, thanks. I guess our ship has come in with a bonanza of good questions." She sincerely hoped there were a few to show him. "I'll haul these home and sort them this weekend."

"Okay."

She was relieved by his indifference to the flood of mail, but riled by his willingness to let her handle it alone. It was so typical of a man to let secretarial tasks fall to a woman.

When he went out for lunch, she got a cheese sandwich from the vending machine and avidly pounced on some letters. In the sampling she had time to read, the advice was well-intentioned and, in the better ones, downright practical. Others raised her hackles: *Make him feel good about himself.*

This reader didn't have a clue about the exceedingly healthy state of Joe's ego.

Defer to his opinions. Yuck! *Tell him how you feel.* She'd already spread out her emotions like a parachute opening in the wind, so why wouldn't he admit he'd read her special column? Was he trying to wiggle out of having a personal relationship? Was he skittish about emotional commitment?

Before Joe got back, she stowed the letters in the trunk of her car.

He took a two-hour lunch break, and they finished the afternoon with a minimum of conversation. He disappeared again shortly before quitting time.

Usually she didn't pay much attention to the activity in the newsroom, but something odd was happening a few minutes before five. Everyone was congregating by the window across from her cubicle. She tried to ignore the commotion, but curiosity got the best of her again.

Across the way, a sign was going up on a billboard, replacing a faded old ad for a local FM radio station, another of William III's enterprises. She stared openmouthed at the bold black letters on bright yellow paper going up in vertical strips. So far, the sign read,

DEAR AM
I
WILL YO
JO

"It's some kind of letter," one of the sportswriters said.

"*M,* space, *O,O,*" Roberta read, giving Amy a peculiar look.

The man on the scaffold added another strip, then another, and Amy was truly speechless for the first time in her life. She couldn't have moved from the spot if an earthquake had rocked the building.

DEAR AMY,
I LOVE YOU.
WILL YOU MARRY ME?
JOE

She felt hands on her shoulders, and the crowd at the window dispersed. It seemed like only seconds before the newsroom was deserted.

Except for Joe.

"What do you think of billboard advertising now?" he asked softly. "Even someone you work with can have a romantic side."

Her throat constricted; her chest tightened. Speech was beyond her.

"Come with me," he said in a voice that gave her goose bumps.

He took her hand and somehow her feet knew enough to go along with him.

"Going up," he said, leading her onto the elevator and using a key for the fourth floor.

"No one goes to the top. That's William III's private suite."

"He lent me a key."

"He helped you do the billboard, didn't he? Is this another publicity stunt, Joe?"

"It's definitely not motivated by any desire on my part to sell more newspapers, sweetheart."

The elevator door opened, and he ushered her into another world, where the carpets were too good to walk on and paintings by artists she could recognize hung on the walls.

"I can't believe it's not just publicity for the column," she said in a shocked voice, not reassured by his disclaimer.

"We don't need more right now. Your appeal for advice put us on the top of the heap. Why do you think our esteemed publisher gave me his space on the billboard and offered to let us use his private suite for some personal business? He had a theory or two of his own on how you should get me back.''

''You did read the column!''

''You knew I did. It didn't take the deductive skills of Sherlock Holmes to notice the paper folded on my desk for two days.''

''Why did you torture me by not saying anything?''

''I wanted to orchestrate a grand gesture, something as romantic as what you did for me when you made a public confession and begged for help. I wouldn't have had the guts to do that. It took me a while to come up with one.''

He led her into the room and closed the door behind them.

''The world's largest coffee table,'' he joked, gesturing at a huge, low, circular piece of furniture with a wooden top polished to mirrorlike brilliance. Half of the upholstered chairs grouped around it were black and the rest were dark burgundy leather. Two matching couches, the longest she'd ever seen, sat at right angles along the rattan-textured corner wall.

''Why are we here?'' The room was so intimidating that she automatically whispered.

''William III thought the newsroom was too public for a verbal proposal of marriage.''

''I'm beginning to think he thought up the whole thing.''

''No, I have to give him credit for the use of the billboard and the room—and for suggesting we write a book based on the columns—but the rest is my idea.''

''You're going too fast—what's this about a book—I can't believe—''

He took her in his arms and covered her mouth with his, making her forget everything but the breadth of his shoulders and the sweetness of his kisses.

She kicked off her heels and stood on tiptoe, molding her form to his, her heart racing with happiness.

"Oh, baby." He clutched her bottom and lifted her against him, his breath ragged and his mouth demanding.

How had they gotten to the couch? She sank under him on cool leather cushions.

"You're slippery." He nuzzled her throat and did wonderful things with the tip of his tongue.

"My panty hose..."

"I'll take that as an invitation."

He rose above her and peeled until there was nothing between her lower half and cold leather. Then he stood and shed his clothes, leaving only his unbuttoned shirt hanging seductively over his lean hips.

"You planned this," she said, surprisingly in awe of the man who urgently wanted to possess her.

"I had high hopes, but part of your charm is I'm never absolutely sure of you."

He did his preparations and came to her, content to reach under her knit top and cup her satin-covered breasts until she cried out in eagerness.

They made love quickly but not frantically, with the confidence of lovers making a beginning, anticipating a lifetime of love.

"I can't believe..." She heard words but didn't know she was saying them.

"I love you, Patterson. I'm crazy about you."

He collapsed on her, and his weight was like a blanket, engulfing and warming her, the varied textures of his skin a sensual feast.

"I love you, Malone."

He managed, with a minimum of wiggling, to reverse their positions and cradle her head in the crook of his arm, holding her there with his long legs and strong arms.

"What's your answer?" he murmured close to her ear.

"Yes."

"Yes to marrying me?"

"Was there another question on the agenda?"

"None important to me."

"Will someone come and find us here?"

"I can't guarantee no one will. If I rushed you—"

"You can't rush someone who's been in love with you since high school."

"You're putting me on."

"Maybe, maybe not. Anyway, I will marry you."

"Good—very good—even excellent."

"If it doesn't work out, our being a husband-and-wife team at work, I'll quit my job."

"I won't let you."

"You won't 'let' me?"

"I'll quit, too."

"Is that what being in love means?" She giggled with happiness.

"I don't think we need to worry. I've discovered the secret of working with you."

"Ignoring me and doing your writing at home?" She was still a tiny bit miffed about that.

"No, getting lots of exercise chasing you around the watercooler."

"Works for me."

"I'm stuck to the couch," he said. "Let's go home."

"Our romantic interlude is over?"

"It's just beginning. I meant, go home together."

He got up, taking her with him, and gave her a small foreshadowing of the night to come.

"I have a wonderful idea for a new series," she murmured.

"If it has anything to do with our sex life, forget it."

He made the back of her throat tickle.

"A series on planning our wedding," she said when she could speak.

He groaned and nipped at her earlobe.

"I thought we could elope—Las Vegas," he said.

"Too tacky. Just think of all the material we'll get if we have a really big—"

"Honeymoon!"

"That, too. Are we really in William III's good graces?" she asked.

"We're his fair-haired wonder kids this week."

"Let's negotiate for a better office."

"Bigger, more space?"

"Solid walls and a door that locks."

"I think this partnership will work, Patterson."

* * * * *

FORTUNE'S Children™

Bestselling Author
MERLINE
LOVELACE

Continues the twelve-book series—FORTUNE'S CHILDREN
in September 1996 with Book Three

BEAUTY AND THE BODYGUARD

Ex-mercenary Rafe Stone was Fortune Cosmetics cover girl
Allie Fortune's best protection against an obsessed stalker. He
was also the one man this tempting beauty was willing to risk
her heart for....

MEET THE FORTUNES—a family whose legacy is greater than
riches. Because where there's a will...there's a *wedding!*

A CASTING CALL TO
ALL FORTUNE'S CHILDREN FANS!
If you are truly one of the fortunate
few, you may win a trip to
Los Angeles to audition for
Wheel of Fortune®. Look for
details in all retail Fortune's Children titles!

WHEEL OF FORTUNE is a registered trademark of Califon Productions, Inc.©
1996 Califon Productions, Inc. All Rights Reserved.

Look us up on-line at: http://www.romance.net

FC-3-C-R

Your very favorite Silhouette miniseries
characters now have a BRAND-NEW story in

CHRISTMAS KISSES

Brought to you by:

LINDA HOWARD

DEBBIE MACOMBER

LINDA TURNER

LINDA HOWARD celebrates the holidays with a **Mackenzie**
wedding—once Maris regains her memory, that is....

DEBBIE MACOMBER brings **Those Manning Men** and
The Manning Sisters home for a mistletoe marriage as
a single dad finally says "I do."

LINDA TURNER brings **The Wild West** alive as
Priscilla Rawlings ties the knot at the Double R Ranch.

Three BRAND-NEW holiday love stories...by romance fiction's
most beloved authors.

Available in November at your favorite retail outlet.

Silhouette®

Look us up on-line at: http://www.romance.net   XMAS96

This October, be the first to read these wonderful
authors as they make their dazzling debuts!

Women to Watch

THE WEDDING KISS by Robin Wells
(Silhouette Romance #1185)
A reluctant bachelor rescues the woman he loves
from the man she's about to marry—and turns into
a willing groom himself!

THE SEX TEST by Patty Salier
(Silhouette Desire #1032)
A pretty professor learns there's more to making love
than meets the eye when she takes lessons from
a sexy stranger.

IN A FAMILY WAY by Julia Mozingo
(Special Edition #1062)
A woman without a past finds shelter in the arms of
a handsome rancher. Can she trust him to protect
her unborn child?

UNDER COVER OF THE NIGHT by Roberta Tobeck
(Intimate Moments #744)
A rugged government agent encounters the woman he has
always loved. But past secrets could threaten their future.

DATELESS IN DALLAS by Samantha Carter
(Yours Truly)
A hapless reporter investigates how to find the perfect
mate—and winds up falling for her handsome rival!

Don't miss the brightest stars of tomorrow!

Only from Silhouette®

Look us up on-line at: http://www.romance.net

WTW

Who can resist a Texan...or a Calloway?

This September, award-winning author
ANNETTE BROADRICK
returns to Texas, with a brand-new
story about the Calloways...

SONS OF TEXAS

Rogues and Ranchers

CLINT: The brave leader. Used to keeping secrets.

CADE: The Lone Star Stud. Used to having women
fall at his feet...

MATT: The family guardian. Used to handling
trouble...

They must discover the identity of the mystery
woman with Calloway eyes—and uncover a
conspiracy that threatens their family....

Look for **SONS OF TEXAS**: Rogues and Ranchers
in September 1996!

Only from Silhouette...where passion lives.

SONSST

Listen to whispers of sweet romance with

Best of the Best™ Audio

Order now for your listening pleasure!

#15295   FIRE AND ICE
$11.99 U.S. ☐ $14.99 CAN. ☐
Written by Janet Dailey.
Read by Erin Gray.

#15292   THE ARISTOCRAT
$11.99 U.S. ☐ $14.99 CAN. ☐
Written by Catherine Coulter.
Read by Marcia Strassman.

#15293   RAGGED RAINBOWS
$11.99 U.S. ☐ $14.99 CAN. ☐
Written by Linda Lael Miller.
Read by Erin Gray.

#15294   THE MAIN ATTRACTION
$11.99 U.S. ☐ $14.99 CAN. ☐
Written by Jayne Ann Krentz.
Read by Marcia Strassman.

(limited quantities available on certain titles)

TOTAL AMOUNT	$
POSTAGE & HANDLING	$
($1.00 for one audio, 50¢ for each additional)	
APPLICABLE TAXES*	$
TOTAL PAYABLE	$
(check or money order— please do not send cash)	

To order, complete this form and send it, along with a check or money order for the total above, payable to Best of the Best Audio, to: **In the U.S.:** 3010 Walden Avenue, P.O. Box 9077, Buffalo, NY 14269-9077; **In Canada:** P.O. Box 636, Fort Erie, Ontario, L2A 5X3.

Name:_____

Address:_____ City:_____

State/Prov.:_____ Zip/Postal Code:_____

*New York residents remit applicable sales taxes. Canadian residents remit applicable GST and provincial taxes.

Available wherever audio books are sold. AUDB

SILHOUETTE... Where Passion Lives

Order these Silhouette favorites today!
Now you can receive a discount by ordering two or more titles!

SD#05890	TWO HEARTS, SLIGHTLY USED by Dixie Browning	$2.99 U.S. ☐	/$3.50 CAN. ☐	
SD#05899	DARK INTENTIONS by Carole Buck	$2.99 U.S. ☐	/$3.50 CAN. ☐	
IM#07604	FUGITIVE FATHER by Carla Cassidy	$3.50 U.S. ☐	/$3.99 CAN. ☐	
IM#07673	THE LONER by Linda Turner	$3.75 U.S. ☐	/$4.25 CAN. ☐	
SSE#09934	THE ADVENTURER by Diana Whitney	$3.50 U.S. ☐	/$3.99 CAN. ☐	
SSE#09867	WHEN STARS COLLIDE by Patricia Coughlin	$3.50 U.S. ☐		
SR#19079	THIS MAN AND THIS WOMAN by Lucy Gordon	$2.99 U.S. ☐	/$3.50 CAN. ☐	
SR#19060	FATHER IN THE MIDDLE by Phyllis Halldorson	$2.99 U.S. ☐	/$3.50 CAN. ☐	
YT#52001	WANTED: PERFECT PARTNER by Debbie Macomber	$3.50 U.S. ☐	/$3.99 CAN. ☐	
YT#52008	HUSBANDS DON'T GROW ON TREES by Kasey Michaels	$3.50 U.S. ☐	/$3.99 CAN. ☐	

(Limited quantities available on certain titles.)

TOTAL AMOUNT	$ _____
DEDUCT: 10% DISCOUNT FOR 2+ BOOKS	$ _____
POSTAGE & HANDLING	$ _____
($1.00 for one book, 50¢ for each additional)	
APPLICABLE TAXES*	$ _____
TOTAL PAYABLE	$ _____
(check or money order—please do not send cash)	

To order, complete this form and send it, along with a check or money order
for the total above, payable to Silhouette Books, to: **In the U.S.:** 3010 Walden
Avenue, P.O. Box 9077, Buffalo, NY 14269-9077; **In Canada:** P.O. Box 636,
Fort Erie, Ontario, L2A 5X3.

Name:_____

Address:_____City:_____

State/Prov.:_____ Zip/Postal Code:_____

*New York residents remit applicable sales taxes.
Canadian residents remit applicable GST and provincial taxes.

SBACK-SN3

V Silhouette®
TM